DEDICATION

To Kris Palmisano with my thanks,
and to Paul, with love.

CHAPTER ONE

Dawn Matheson stood under the roof of the ferry's upper deck huddled against the corner trying to stay out of the cold October rain. The ferry had tipped and rolled and chopped into the churning whitecaps of Lake Superior since the trip from Big Bay on the mainland began 25 minutes earlier. Its icy water sprayed onto the deck and splashed over the rails. Feeling seasick, Dawn choked down the nausea creeping into her throat.

When the ferry suddenly slammed into a wave, she lost her footing and tilted sideways. Luckily, her husband Noel caught her by the waist before she could fall. He was six feet tall and still built like the football player he'd been in high school 15 years earlier.

"We're almost there," he said, standing her upright and pointing through a break in the mist. "Wolf Island is straight ahead."

Dawn was a petite five-foot-three, slender, and weighed 110 pounds dripping wet. Although she was dressed warmly in jeans, a down jacket, gloves, a scarf, and a knit cap over her curly, shoulder-length copper hair, a shiver ran the length of her. Whether from the bad weather conditions or the first glimpse of her new town, she wasn't sure.

1

"Wolf Island," Noel repeated. "Home sweet home."

She cut him a sideways glance. "Are you sure this is a good idea?" She looped her arm through his, partly to keep from falling again, but mostly because she needed reassurance and comfort. "We can still change our minds."

His brown-eyed gaze jerked to her. "No, we can't." As if he recognized he'd been too curt, he smiled and patted her hand. "It'll be fine, you'll see. It's not like we're moving to another country where they speak a different language. This is where I grew up. Everyone on the island knows me."

"All two hundred and forty-six residents, right?" She battled to keep her voice light while feeling her heart drop. She was a city girl and had never lived anywhere but Chicago. Moving to a small island 14 miles long and 3 miles wide in the middle of Lake Superior *was* like another country and would take some getting used to.

"Make that two hundred and forty-eight residents, as of today," Noel replied. His lips lifted in a crooked grin. With his broad shoulders squared and his proud chin jutting forward, he stared ahead to the waterfront village of Thunder Point as the ferry drew near.

"But I don't know anyone," she reminded him. "I left everyone and everything familiar back in Chicago, including my job." She felt on the verge of tears, a feeling that had come easily for months.

When she squeezed his arm his head turned, and his eyes looked as hard as marbles. "This will be good for you. We agreed upon it."

Dawn inhaled a deep breath of frigid air. She hadn't much choice in the matter, unless she divorced

2

Noel and forged a life on her own. After only three years of marriage, she wasn't willing to throw in the towel. The vows they'd taken were sacred to her: for better or worse, for richer or poorer, in sickness and in health until death did they part.

They'd certainly faced challenges regarding that last promise. Her inability to bring a child to term was the primary reason they'd uprooted their lives to move to Wolf Island.

The events that had led to this day rolled through her mind.

Six months ago, a message came from Noel's estranged brother, Keith, by way of a private investigator. Their parents were dead, killed in a hit and run accident. An elderly woman had suffered a heart attack behind the wheel, ran them down on the street, and crashed into another parked vehicle—unoccupied, fortunately. The three involved died instantaneously. Although Dawn wanted to go with him to attend his parents' funeral, Noel insisted on traveling alone. He didn't feel she was up to the journey, as she'd recently experienced her second miscarriage.

When he returned from the funeral, he informed her that he'd met with a lawyer to hear the will. The brothers had inherited their parents' house, but Keith didn't want it.

Noel made several trips back in the next few months to handle the estate and ready the house for sale.

Much to Dawn's surprise, when he returned home from the last trip, he announced that he'd bought Keith out, was not selling the house, and he'd decided a move to Wolf Island would be in their best interest.

She recalled the heated argument that followed.

"You must be joking. We can't drop everything and leave Chicago. Our life is here. We have jobs, friends and our condo."

"Things aren't working here, Dawn," he'd said, in a flash of temper.

"What do you mean by that?"

"You know perfectly well." His hands balled at his sides. "I'm going nowhere in my job. We have no sex life anymore. I thought we'd have a family by now. We need a change. *I* need a change."

Dawn's gaze had dropped to the ground. After two miscarriages in two years, she'd been afraid to try again. Even cuddling with Noel would have led to sex, so she'd avoided any kind of intimacy for months. The pain of losing two babies had been unbearable, not to mention the shame and guilt associated with not being able to bear Noel's child. Feeling helpless and inadequate, she'd battled depression for some time. Their conversation that day seemed the perfect opportunity to make a suggestion she'd been contemplating.

"Why don't we look into adopting?"

"You know how I feel about that," he'd replied, shaking his head. "I want my own kids."

For the first time in a long time, she'd felt deep emotions bubbling to the surface. "There are so many children in this world who need good, loving homes. A baby would be our own the moment he or she was placed in our arms."

"Don't play word games with me, Dawn. You understand what I'm talking about. It's not the same as flesh and blood."

Noel rarely backed down when he thought he was right, which she'd learned was most of the time. Dawn had learned to pick her fights. Knowing this was one she wouldn't come close to winning, she'd sighed and felt tears sting her eyes. "Then, if you're unwilling to adopt, maybe we should just try to accept that we aren't meant to be parents."

Something apparently struck a nerve, because he suddenly gathered her into his arms and pulled her to his chest and spoke gently, his words flowing out in a rush. "Wolf Island is where I grew up. It's a great place to raise a family. The slow pace of life is relaxing, and my folks' house is paid off, so we won't have a mortgage. The cost of living is lower on the island. I've arranged to work remotely, and I even negotiated a small raise that I've been due, so there's no need for you to work anymore. You can concentrate on having a baby. The added stress of working while trying to get pregnant will be gone."

"But I like my job. Working had nothing to do with the miscarriages."

He continued, his voice lifting with excitement. "We've already got a buyer for our condo, and we're going to make a good profit on it. It's a win-win situation."

Dawn couldn't believe her ears. She shoved back from his chest, and her mouth gaped. "You spoke to a realtor about selling our condo?"

"I didn't want you to worry about the details. It's practically a done deal. All we have to do is sign on the dotted line."

"But you went behind my back. How could you do that? We're supposed to be a team and make decisions together." It felt like she'd been punched in the stomach.

Noel's lips pursed, something she'd noticed him doing more of lately. "We can't continue like this. You and I both know it. Something has to change if we're going to remain in this marriage, so I took the initiative and made something happen. Do you want to stay married and move to Wolf Island, or do you want a divorce?"

The ultimatum had nearly knocked the wind out of her. "Would you really divorce me because I can't bear your child?"

Noel's face had gone white, and his eyes grew large. Maybe he'd heard the shock and hurt in her voice and it finally knocked some sense into him. "Of course not, honey, but I promise you're going to love Wolf Island. Thunder Point is a charming little town with nice people. You'll make friends, and you'll love the peace and quiet of my childhood home."

Tears washed her cheeks. "I didn't even meet your parents or visit where you grew up in the three years we've been married. Why is that? I've never understood."

"My parents were elderly and unable to travel. I explained that to you numerous times. They had Keith and me later in life."

"Then why didn't we go to Wolf Island to see them? I wanted to know them. They were my in-laws. Didn't they want to meet me?"

"Sure they did, but that first year we were newlyweds and I wanted you all to myself. We had our jobs that kept us both busy. You know how hard I've worked to get ahead, not that it's gotten me anywhere," he grumbled. "And then there were...your health issues."

She'd winced. He'd made it sound like she was an invalid. "Losing a baby isn't the same as having health problems," she'd responded, choking back emotion.

"I didn't mean it that way. It's just that, well, it happened twice and then…"

"Then what?"

"You've been so blue ever since."

Her temper sparked, which had been a rare occurrence in the year that had passed. "Yes, Noel, I've been blue. I'm sure I'm not the only woman to become depressed after having a miscarriage, and as you pointed out, I've had two." Her words bit, but she didn't care. Her life had been turned upside down and now he was flipping it again.

"I know how badly you want to be a mother," he'd said. "I thought I was doing the right thing by offering you an environment with a more laid-back lifestyle. But if you want to stay in Chicago, we'll stay. I'll put the house on Wolf Island up for sale and, somehow, I'll get us out of the condo contract."

When he pulled her to him again, she laid her head on his chest and sobbed. After a couple of minutes, she'd regained composure. "If you think we can grow close again by moving to Wolf Island, I'm willing to relocate. I love you. I don't want a divorce."

It had been a whirlwind of activity since, and now they were here.

The ferry captain's voice boomed over the loud speaker. "All ashore who is going ashore!"

Dawn's heartbeat sped up as Noel took her hand. Fortunately, the rain stopped just in time to disembark, and the sun peeked through the clouds, providing a brighter view of the shops lining Main Street beyond the ferry landing. Her stomach was still a bit queasy, but as soon as her feet touched solid ground, she'd feel better.

"Here we are," Noel said, as the ferry docked. "Ready to get the car and see your new home?"

She nodded, not knowing anything about Noel's parents' house except that it was located outside the Thunder Point town limits, set in the woods. That thought already had her nerves on edge. She was used to the city with its skyline, crowds, and noises.

As they filed behind other passengers walking down the ramp, she noticed Noel's gaze shifting over the small crowd of people waiting onshore.

"Who are you looking for?" she asked.

"Huh? No one. I'm wondering which side the cars will be unloading on."

"Probably the side that leads to the parking lot." She pointed to the cars already being driven off the ferry, wondering why he wouldn't know that already. He'd come across from the mainland on the same ferry numerous times in recent months.

He chuckled. "You're so smart."

"Is that why you married me?"

With a wink, he replied, "No, I married you for your money. You know that."

Dawn nudged his rib with her elbow. "Funny." He'd made that joke plenty of times before, and it was getting old. The truth was she did have money, twice as much as he'd brought into the marriage. Her father had owned a successful marketing and PR firm in Chicago that he sold shortly before dying five years earlier. Since Dawn's mom had passed away when

Dawn was thirteen, Dawn inherited their entire estate. She was well-to-do and had purchased their condo, as well as most of the furnishings, with her money. Aside from those investments, she preferred they live modestly on their middle-class incomes, keeping her inheritance safely squirreled away for an emergency or old age.

"There's our car," she said, seeing the Jeep Cherokee driven off the ramp and into the lot. They'd packed it with their clothes, the computer, and a few more personal belongings that would fit. Her in-laws' house was furnished with everything they'd need, Noel had said. Despite Dawn wishing she could have brought more of her own special things to make their home feel like her own, he had convinced her to sell their condo furniture to make life easier. Some items, however, she refused to part with, so they'd been packed in boxes and shipped to the Thunder Point post office.

"When will we pick up our boxes?" she asked, climbing into the passenger seat of the Jeep and noticing the post office was next door to the ferry landing.

"All in good time," he said, slamming the driver's door. "I want to get out to the house before we do anything else so you'll see it while the light is still good." It was three in the afternoon, and even though the rain had slowed to a drizzle, clouds overhead threatened to bring another storm.

He stuck the key in the ignition and the engine turned over. "I'm surprised it started on the first try. It's cold today." He blew on his glove-less hands and cranked up the heat.

9

"I told you to wear gloves," she said. "And a hat. Isn't your head cold? They say body heat goes straight out through your head."

"I'll survive. I've been a Midwesterner all my life."

"I've been one, too, but I still get cold."

"That's because you barely have any meat on your bones. You look like a little scarecrow."

She frowned, a stab of hurt slicing through her at his words. Trauma and depression had led to lack of appetite and weight loss, but Dawn had been trying to add pounds to return to the shapely woman she had been.

As soon as Noel pulled past the Dockside Gift Shop, he pumped on the brakes and jerked to a stop. Two women standing in front of the town gazebo had caught his attention. They waved and he waved back.

"Who are they?" Dawn inquired.

"Two old classmates." He rolled down his window and hollered, "Hi, ladies."

They called back hello in unison.

"Home to stay this time?" one woman asked. She was tall with straight black hair streaming down her back. She wore an elegant fur cap that resembled a pillow box, a deep red leather coat over jeans that molded to her legs, and knee-high black boots with heels.

"Yep, my wife and I are heading out to Mom and Pop's house now." He nodded toward Dawn but didn't introduce her. Instinctively, she lifted her hand in a polite wave.

"Good to see you again," the other female said. She was about a half-foot shorter than the fur-capped woman and was dressed more casually in a down jacket not unlike Dawn's, corduroy trousers, and hiking boots. Bareheaded, her hair was blonde and cut in a pixie style.

"Catch you guys later," Noel said, rolling up his window. When he started the car moving, he glanced at Dawn. "That was Madeline Reed and Leslie Duvall. I didn't know they were friends. They didn't run with the same crowd in school."

"The cliques that existed in high school usually fade away once people grow up and have been out of school for a while," Dawn noted.

"Anyway, see how nice people are here. You'll make friends in no time."

As he turned right, she took note of the small stores and restaurants on both sides of the street: The Island Market, a café called the Beach Club, a pizza joint named Tony's, a pottery studio, the bank, a real estate office, donut shop, the police station and more. It was surreal. This little town with turn-of-the-century charm was their new home. *Her* new home.

Toto, we're not in Kansas anymore, she thought, doing her best to stay positive.

"There's the beach," Noel said, pointing to the right as he drove out of town.

She pressed her face to the glass and liked what she saw. "It's pretty, even this time of year. I can imagine how nice it'll be in the summer."

"There's a lot to do here. The island has nine miles of hiking trails, underwater caves to explore, and a lagoon where bald eagles makes nests in pine trees on the cliffs."

"You didn't tell me any of that."

"And there's the boat marina," he continued. "Almost everyone on the island has a boat to use during the warmer seasons."

"Does the lake freeze over in winter?"

"Yes, but before the ice gets too thick for the boats to cross, there's an ice road that can be accessed from the mainland. A wind sled taxi runs on top of the ice. It's pretty fun. I worked as a wind sled taxi driver between Big Bay and Wolf Island when I was in high school."

Dawn's eyes widened. "You never cease to amaze me. Lately, I've been learning something new about you almost every day."

"You know what they say. Mystery is the spice of life," he responded.

After he turned onto Old Fort Road, Dawn saw what looked to be an ancient cemetery.

"That's an old burial site for the Chippewa Indians," Noel said. His eyes were bright and his voice enthusiastic. Pointing out the local sites as if he was a proud tour guide, he sounded happy for the first time in a long time. Perhaps it had been a good idea to move here, after all.

Dawn didn't know much about Wolf Island, but she did remember Noel saying that it had been inhabited by Native Americans, fur traders, and missionaries for over 400 years. So much history.

A little farther ahead, he slowed the Jeep and pointed out her window to an empty field. "Back in the late seventeen hundreds, a fur trading post set in that field. One of the original families to settle on Wolf Island traded furs and farmed there for half a century. It's private property now."

As they passed the field, she noticed a post stuck in the ground with a brass plate on top. Too bad that was the only thing to mark history. She wanted to ask more about the cemetery, because this was the most animated Noel had been in months, but she suddenly felt very tired. "How far is it to the house?"

"Just down this road another mile."

When he made a turn off the main road onto a gravel driveway, she felt the hairs on the back of her neck bristle. They were surrounded by dense, dark woods on both sides. As if on cue, the rain began to fall again the moment he stopped in front of the house. Dawn sat up straighter in her seat and stared out the front windshield at the view she could only describe as gloomy.

"Is this it?" she asked.

"This is it."

The farmhouse was two stories with a pitched tin roof and covered porches with railings that stretched across the front on both levels. The clapboard siding was a dingy gray color, but had probably been white— many years ago. Even from this distance, it was evident the exterior was chipped and could use sanding and a fresh coat of paint. What she guessed might be an added-on sun porch jutted from one side of the house. On the other side of the house set a detached garage and an old shed.

A tall, ancient looking oak tree stood in the front yard guarding the place like a sentry; branches shrouded in mist reached to the sky. Most of the leaves had already fallen and lay in wet piles on the ground, rendering the scene even more dismal.

"The original part of the house was built in

13

eighteen ninety-five. Pop was born here," Noel said. "I'm not sure if I told you that or not."

He'd told her very little about his hometown and family. She glanced at the woods that surrounded the house and felt her pulse quicken. "I didn't know it would be so isolated." *Or old*, she thought.

"You'll get used to it. Don't think of it so much as isolated, but as private."

They sat for a few moments staring at the house while waiting for the rain to subside. They didn't have an umbrella in the car. Then, something completely unexpected happened. A howl pierced the air so loud they could hear it from inside the car with the rain beating on the roof.

Dawn grabbed Noel's arm. "What was that? A wolf?"

"Can't be. Way back when, wolves regularly migrated from the mainland in the winter, but it's been over one hundred years since there's been any documentation of a wolf on this island. That must have been a neighbor's dog."

Goosebumps peppered her arms. *What neighbor?* They hadn't passed another house in over a mile. Wisconsin could have been Mars for as dissimilar as it was from Chicago. "I'm used to the sounds of the city," she said. "Noises in the country must be something altogether different."

He smiled and squeezed her hand. "Yeah, they're much more interesting. Welcome home, honey."

CHAPTER TWO

When there was a short break in the weather, Dawn and Noel dashed from the car to the house and up the porch stairs. She noticed he'd added the house key to his key ring that also held the key to the Jeep and a couple of others.

"Do you have a second house key for me?" she asked.

"No, there was only one in Mom and Pop's stuff, but we can get one made for you, if you think you'll need it."

"Yes, I'll want one."

He stuck the key in the lock and turned the knob. When he pushed the door open it creaked, just like in a horror movie, and they were met with darkness.

"I hope the power is still on," Noel said.

"What?" Her voice lifted an octave. Didn't you take care of that?" What would they do if there was no electricity? Would they have to search in the dark for candles and flashlights? They'd freeze to death without heat.

He chuckled. "I'm just teasing. Don't you think I made sure the power would be on? It's already in my name. I took care of it the last time I was here."

"Don't you mean, in our name?"

"Well, sure. That's what I meant." His hand moved inside the door to the wall. With the flick of a switch, the foyer was bathed in light.

Dawn breathed a sigh of relief.

They stepped inside and Noel closed the door behind them. "Well, here we are."

They stood side-by-side, silent, as she gazed around the space. Oak paneling covered the foyer walls, and a well-constructed oak staircase rose in front of them leading to the second level. The floors were hardwood— more oak. Despite the ceiling light, the entry was dim and felt closed in, opposite from their contemporary condo that had an open floor plan and huge windows that overlooked the Chicago River. She'd fallen in love with the condo because of the natural light.

"So, this is where I grew up," he said, taking her hand. "Let me give you the grand tour."

The first stop was a small room to the right of the stairs. Noel flipped on the light to reveal a leather recliner, a bookcase filled with trophies, a wooden desk sitting under a window, an older box-style television sitting on a table against one wall, and a gun rack on the opposite wall. The top half of the walls were papered in a masculine green and red stripe pattern, and the lower half was in oak wainscoting. "This was Pop's man cave, as if you couldn't tell."

When her gaze met the glassy eyes of a deer mounted on the wall, Dawn jumped. "Did your father kill that animal?"

"Yeah, he hunted, just like all of the men in Thunder Point. There are a lot of deer in the woods around us."

"Did you hunt, too, when you lived here?"

"Sure. Pop bought Keith and me our first rifles when we were twelve years old."

That was another surprise. "I had no idea," she said. "You haven't told me much of anything about your childhood." The sophisticated and stylish man she'd met in Chicago and been married to for three years didn't match the image of the country boy who had grown up in this farmhouse.

He pointed to the gun rack. "These rifles and shotguns are all loaded. Don't touch them unless you're prepared to pull the trigger."

"I wouldn't! Guns scare me. Do we have to keep them?"

"I might want to take up hunting again. I cleaned them all the last time I was here and stocked up on ammo."

"Really?" He'd never even gone to a shooting range since they'd been married, that she knew of. Loaded guns in the house definitely made her uncomfortable, but that was something they could discuss later.

Down the hall was a bathroom, not updated as she'd hoped. It looked to be stuck in the 1950s. Next, they stepped into a room Noel described as the family room. A plaid couch set against one wall. Two chairs in gold fabric flanked either side of the sofa, and a television set against the opposite wall. Surprisingly, this TV was a flat screen. The walls themselves may have been painted a light green or blue at one time, but now they looked pale gray.

Off the family room was a screened-in sun porch, as Dawn had guessed from the car. She opened the

French doors dividing it from the family room and stepped inside. With the rain coming down and the wind cutting through the trees, the view of the woods outside the windows was downright spooky. Cold air blew through the window screens. Although she was wearing warm clothes, she shivered, not so much from the cold, but from remembering the howl they'd heard. If it had been a dog, she hoped it didn't have rabies. She didn't want it coming near the house at all. She'd never had a pet and had no desire to be in contact with any animals, let alone wild ones.

"You might like to read out here in the daytime," Noel said. "This was Mom's favorite spot. It's not a four-season room, as you can tell, but I remember she often sat out here in the fall with a blanket over her legs." He stared at the wicker loveseat adorned with a floral padded seat that looked old and bleached out. The loveseat was accessorized with two throw pillows with the same floral pattern. The only other furniture in the room was a white rocking chair and a small glass-topped table with iron legs. All the furniture set on top of a large oval braided rug that looked to be in need of a good vacuum. The porch floor was constructed of wide planks that had been painted dark brown.

"I'm sure it's a nice spot when the sun's shining," Dawn replied, politely, though the floral fabric wasn't her style at all and the old pad would have to be replaced before she sat on the loveseat.

When she saw that Noel hadn't moved and his gaze was riveted to the loveseat, she jiggled his arm. "Are you all right?"

"Huh?" He snapped out of his trance and turned toward her. "Yeah, I'm fine."

"Are you thinking about your parents?"

"I guess so." He chewed on his lower lip and seemed to be contemplating something.

"You must miss them. It had been a long time since you were all together."

He nodded. "This might sound strange, but I can feel her in this room."

Dawn's eyebrow arched. Her gaze shifted around the porch, praying not to see a ghostly figure hovering in the corner. "Who? Your mother?"

"Yes." He met Dawn's wide-eyed gaze and smiled, apparently reading her mind. "Don't worry. She didn't die in the house, you know. All I mean is that she loved her home, but she especially enjoyed this sun porch. It's where she was the happiest. Pop and I built the room for her when I was a sophomore in high school."

"What about your brother? Did he help, too?"

Noel's brows winged down. "No. Keith spent most his high school years drinking and smoking dope, and running with a wild bunch of hoodlums. He was rarely at home, let alone bother to help with anything around the farm."

"Is that why you two don't get along? Surely he's grown up now and changed his ways."

"A leopard doesn't change his spots." Noel flicked the porch light off and prodded her through the door with his hand on the small of her back. "I don't want to talk about him. I'll show you the rest of the house."

"All right." She'd known better than to bring up Keith, but there were so many blank spaces regarding Noel's life. He'd been a private person when they met, and not having had much dating experience, she'd

19

found that quality mysterious and interesting at the time. Unfortunately, nothing much had changed in three years. She still knew little about what really made her husband tick. Now that they were back on his old stomping grounds, she hoped that would change. As he'd said, everyone knew him in Thunder Point. Dawn was hopeful that some of them would be happy to tell her stories from his past. Perhaps she'd even find out the real reason why he hadn't been home in so many years prior to his parents passing away.

They toured the living room on the other side of the house, which was furnished with more well-worn furniture and wallpapered in a green and white leaf design. Obviously, decorating had not been his mother's specialty. The room's saving grace was the floor-to-ceiling stone fireplace that filled one wall, complete with a thick primitive-style oak mantle, which Dawn immediately swooned over.

Above the mantle hung a large oil painting. The man in the portrait sat in a cushioned chair. His wife stood at his side with her hand resting on his shoulder.

"Those are my folks," Noel said. "Apparently, they posed about five years ago for a local artist. The painting was something my mother always wanted. I'm glad she finally got it."

Dawn stared at the couple in the portrait, recognizing physical traits of Noel in both. In his father, Noel had inherited the same square jaw and high forehead. Noel's eye shape and smile came from his mother. In this painting, her silver hair was cut in a bobbed style, and she wore a blue dress with small white polka dots and a lace collar. It might have been her Sunday-go-to-church dress.

"They look like a very nice couple," she observed, wishing again that she'd met them.

The next stop was the kitchen. It was large but as outdated as she expected. Wooden painted cabinets with ceramic knobs, laminate countertops, and a linoleum floor were as unattractive as the old white appliances. The only charming feature was the original farm sink. There was no formal dining room in the house. The kitchen was eat-in, which was fine, since Dawn didn't expect to be hosting big gatherings. There was no family to invite to share holidays with—and no friends, either. Chasing away somber thoughts, she slid her over palm across the dining table with its butcher-block top. She liked it and the spindle chairs shoved underneath that looked antique.

"Do you think you can whip up your famous pecan waffles in this kitchen?" Noel joked.

She shrugged, deciding right then that she'd be dipping into her nest egg to renovate not only the kitchen, but the entire house. All the rooms needed a lot of TLC. Either that or they'd have to sell the place and move. Even though she was sure Mr. and Mrs. Matheson had been wonderful people, this was not a home that felt welcoming and warm. It was not her style at all.

Noel didn't want her to work, but she had to do something or she'd go crazy. A renovation project would be the perfect solution. However, she'd wait a while to tell him. There was no use in starting an argument.

He led her up the stairs to a carpeted hallway and pointed to the closed bedroom door on the right. "That was Keith's room. Mine was in the back."

When they stepped into what had been Noel's bedroom, Dawn was shocked to find that it was empty. There was not a stick of furniture inside, and not even a rug on the floor. No pictures hung on the walls or curtains at the windows. He'd moved out years earlier, but an extra room would normally be used for guests or storage.

He must have noticed her surprise. "Mom and Pop were getting ready to paint this room when they were killed. That's what their lawyer told me. They'd packed whatever stuff was left from my childhood and put it in storage, including the furniture."

"Oh. I wonder what they were planning to use the space for."

He shrugged. "Can't imagine. Maybe they just wanted to freshen it up."

The walls looked dingy, like the rest of the house. She wondered why they'd bother to paint a room that wasn't used anymore, as opposed to one of the public areas, but she didn't bother to ask. She was trying hard to be positive, but it was difficult not to feel disappointed with the whole house.

Noel squeezed her waist. "Since this room is a blank canvas, we could redo it and make it a nursery." His brow arched, and their eyes locked. It seemed he was waiting for a retort of some kind.

She stiffened under his touch. They'd just arrived and he was already starting! Before she could respond, he grabbed her hand and tugged her past a full bathroom that had pink tiles and a claw foot tub, which she had to admit she'd enjoy. It was deep and roomy, and she could imagine steaming bubble baths on a cold winter's night.

Next, they stepped into a large bedroom that had obviously been his parents' room.

Their iron bed was against one wall, with a colorful patch quilt still covering the mattress. Even their pillows were propped where their heads had last lay upon them. The thought of sleeping in his parents' bed and on their pillows gave her the willies. It was a good thing she'd thought to throw their own feather pillows into the Jeep, as well as a set of sheets and a couple of blankets.

A painting of a log cabin in the woods next to a lake hung above the bed. A cedar hope chest set at the end of the bed on another old rug that needed to be thrown away. A tall dresser, another bureau with a rectangular mirror above it, and a slider rocker with a hassock in front of it filled the rest of the room. She hoped Noel had removed his folks' clothes from the dressers on one of his trips. Surely he had. That wouldn't be a job she'd relish.

Heavy drapes hung from windows that would probably let a lot of light in if allowed. Dawn vowed to pull down the drapes as soon as she could and replace them with light and airy curtains.

"Well, that's it. You've seen everything. What do you think of the house?" Noel asked. He sat on the bed, which squeaked under his weight, and patted the space beside him. When she remained frozen to her spot, he said, "I know it's not what you're used to, but with a few of your special touches, you can make it your own."

Her spirit brightened. "Do you mean it, Noel? Because I was thinking we could renovate. It's a charming house, but every room could use updating."

23

When he frowned, she quickly added, "I have the money to pay for a renovation, and it'll give me something to do since you don't want me to work."

He jolted up, rigid as a board. "We're not going to use your inheritance to renovate a perfectly good house. We can remove some of the furniture if you'd like, and hire someone to paint the rooms, but have you forgotten I'm going to be working from home now? I can't have the place in disarray for months on end with carpenters, plumbers, and electricians making a racket."

Naturally, he was the beneficiary of her share of their combined assets, but she wanted to remind Noel that she could do as she pleased with her inheritance money. It had been *her* father's money after all—earned from his hard work. However, moving to Wolf Island was supposed to be a fresh start for them. This battle she'd fight later, because it was not something she would give in to. If she was going to live here, she had to feel comfortable, and that meant a huge makeover. But it was getting late, she was hungry and tired, and it wasn't worth an argument right now. She changed the subject.

"Can we go into town to grab a bite before we unpack the car? It's been a long day and I'm starving."

"Really? I haven't heard those words from you in ages." His eyes narrowed, probably wondering why she wasn't making more of a fuss about renovating, but he didn't say anything else. "I'm hungry, too. You know I need three square meals a day." He pulled the drape back from the window. "Look, the rain has stopped."

"Good, but it's pretty chilly in the house. Can you turn up the heat before we go so it'll be warm when we get back?"

"Of course."

They went downstairs and Noel adjusted the thermostat. "There are probably logs cut and stacked in the shed outside. I can start a fire in the fireplace when we return, if you'd like."

"That would be nice." She would love to snuggle with her husband in front of a cozy fire, as long as it didn't lead to him wanting to make love. Her heart started to beat faster just thinking about it. This might be a new beginning for them, but she still wasn't ready for that.

****

When they entered the Beach Club Café and found seats at a corner table, Noel and the waitress greeted each other by first name. She was an attractive young woman who appeared to be in her twenties. Curious, Dawn's eyebrow lifted.

"He eats here a lot," the bored-looking girl explained, pen poised over her notepad.

"I came here for supper almost every night on my trips back," Noel clarified.

Dawn nodded and perused the menu.

They had just placed their orders for burgers and fries when the raven-haired woman they'd seen at the ferry landing walked in, accompanied by a stocky man with a bald head and goatee. Noel's back was to the door and he was scrolling through his phone. Dawn touched his hand and whispered, "Your old school friend is here."

"Who?" He twisted in his chair and said, "Oh, it's Madeline."

Her gaze met his, and he waved the couple over. When they approached, he stood up and gave her a hug. "Are you stalking me, Maddie?" he joked. "We've run into each other two times in one day."

She smiled. "No. I don't cook, and you know as well as I do that there aren't many options in Thunder Point."

Dawn was taken aback by the seductive tone of the woman's voice. She practically purred like a cat. She hadn't changed her stylish outfit either, since they saw her earlier. Dawn felt like a toad next to the tall, exotic woman.

Madeline's dark eyes shifted to and over her, before she held out her hand. As Dawn slipped her palm into hers, she was fully aware of the woman's sensuality. It was in the way her head angled, how her eyes narrowed and delved, her full lips tilting in a half-smile...

"We haven't met," she said. "I'm Madeline Reed, and you're Noel's wife." It was a statement, not a question.

"Yes, I'm Dawn. Pleased to meet you. Noel tells me you're old school friends."

She smiled at him. "That's right. It's nice to have him back on the island again. For good this time, we hear."

"That's right. We've relocated, and I'm glad to be back," he replied.

"I'm sorry for your loss," Madeline's companion interjected, speaking to Noel. "You probably don't remember me, because I was about five years ahead of you in school, but I'm Carl Fisher."

It took a moment, but Noel seemed to remember

him. "Oh yeah, Carl Fisher. You played football. How the hell are you?"

They shook hands. "Fine, just fine." His lips, which Dawn noticed were chapped, drew into a solemn line. "It was a tragedy what happened to your folks and Mrs. Whittier, though she probably should have had her driver's license taken away years ago. Did you go after her life insurance company or sue her family?"

Dawn sucked in a breath. What a horrible thing to ask. And people thought Chicagoans were rude.

Noel shook his head. "No, her family was devastated and felt terrible about the whole thing, but it was an accident plain and simple. She had a heart attack. There was no need to drag anyone into court. Mom and Pop wouldn't have wanted that."

Relieved by his response, Dawn smiled and nodded to assure him of her support.

"Carl, this is my wife."

"Pleasure to meet you," he said, reaching for Dawn's hand.

"Same here," she responded, although it really wasn't. She kept her hands firmly under the table on her lap. It probably wasn't fair to judge a person on first impressions, but she didn't care for his attitude.

"Are you two dating?" Noel asked, glancing between the couple.

"Noel, that's really none of our business." Dawn felt her face flush with embarrassment.

"It's all right," Madeline said. "Yes, Carl and I are dating." She chuckled softly and stroked Carl's cheek with her fingernails, which Dawn noticed were long and painted bright red to match her jacket. Then she bumped her hip against his and nipped at his earlobe with her teeth.

"You sexy little cat," Carl replied, slapping her bottom.

The PDA seemed too much for a family café and certainly made Dawn uncomfortable. She cleared her throat and blurted, "Do either of you know if there are wolves in the woods?"

The couple stared at her. Dawn looked at Noel to see him roll his eyes.

Carl answered first. "Although the island got its name because of the wolves that once inhabited it, there haven't been any around here for over a century. Why do you ask?"

"We heard an animal howling in the woods today. I saw a documentary about wolves once, and this animal sounded just like those on the show."

"I told her it was probably an injured dog." Noel drummed his fingers on the table and smiled at the couple. "Dawn has a vivid imagination."

She cut him a glance. "You heard it, too. It didn't sound like a dog to me. It had a unique howl."

"So, you've already been out to the farmhouse?" Madeline asked, changing the subject and addressing Noel.

"Yes, Dawn has seen it."

"What do you think of the property?" Madeline asked her. Her gaze delved deep, her lips pulled into a smirk.

Dawn felt like a bug being studied under a microscope. "It's…quite rustic. I'm glad to finally see where Noel grew up. I'm sure we're going to be happy in Thunder Point." Her words sounded chipper, but inside her heart beat wildly, and she felt that all-too-familiar sense of melancholy flood her body.

Noel lowered his voice in what came across as a conspiratorial whisper. "Dawn thinks my mother might be haunting the house."

Madeline and Carl both barked out a laugh.

Mortified, Dawn's jaw dropped. "I never said that, Noel. You're the one who said you felt her presence on the sun porch."

He reached across the table and touched her hand. "It's okay, honey. We're among friends." He glanced between the couple, and his lips lifted in what could only be described as a smug grin. "Dawn hasn't been feeling well lately. We decided to move here, partly because she needs peace and quiet, and lots of rest."

Stunned, Dawn lowered her gaze to her lap and wrenched her hands together. Why had Noel said such a thing? Madeline and Carl weren't *her* friends. They were strangers, and he'd just portrayed her as mentally unstable, or at the very least, weak and prone to flights of fancy.

"Your secret's safe with us," Madeline purred.

Dawn's head snapped up, and she quietly said, "I have no secrets." She narrowed her eyes at Noel.

"Will you join us?" he asked the couple, ignoring her glare.

"No, we've bothered you long enough," Carl replied. "We'll grab our own booth. Good to see you again."

Noel nodded. "Same here. See you around town."

Madeline flipped her long hair over her shoulder and smiled. "Nice to finally meet you, Dawn."

They said their goodbyes and the couple strolled to the back of the café and slid into a booth.

Dawn began to shake. "Why did you say that

about me?" she asked Noel, quietly. "Do you know how embarrassed I am?"

"I'm sorry. I didn't mean anything by it, but you *do* need rest. You've been through a lot in the past two years."

"What I've been through is nobody's business." She felt so betrayed, she could barely breathe. "And why did Madeline say it was nice to *finally* meet me? What's that supposed to mean?"

"This is a small town and word gets around. People knew we were moving home. I've been gone a lot of years and my friends are glad to finally meet you. Don't take things so personally."

Noel hadn't bothered to introduce her to his family, yet somehow, classmates from years ago knew about her? That didn't add up.

Just then their meals arrived. He began to dig in like he was ravished, but she pushed her plate away.

"Aren't you going to eat?" he asked, dousing his fries with ketchup. "You said you were hungry."

"I've lost my appetite."

He wiped his mouth on a napkin and sighed. "I apologize if I hurt your feelings, but you know how sensitive you've become. *Overly* sensitive about every little thing. I have to walk on eggshells around you and, frankly, it's getting old."

She squeezed her eyes shut and reached for calm. That wasn't true. She'd been too depressed to have been ruffled by anything he said or did for about six months. But she was on the mend now. *He* was the one who seemed to be wound tight these days. Wanting to remind him of that, Dawn kept her mouth shut, knowing it wouldn't help matters to sling mud.

When she re-opened her eyes, she said, "It's been a long day and we're both tired. Let's eat and go home."

"That's more like it. A better attitude will work wonders."

While Noel worked at polishing off everything on his plate in record time, she picked at hers, neither of them speaking.

When they finished, he paid the bill and left a hefty tip on the table, then his gaze flew to the back of the room. Carl and Madeline waved goodbye, and Dawn and Noel politely waved back.

"Madeline certainly is different," she said, as they exited the café and walked to the Jeep. "She's not the kind of person I expected to meet in a town like this."

His head tilted. "A town like this? That's a pretty snobby thing to say, Dawn."

"Sorry, I didn't mean it that way. She's not your run-of-the-mill small town girl. That's all I meant."

He peered into the clear sky illuminated with stars and reminisced. "Well, Maddie always had a flair for the dramatic. She was the star of all the school plays. It was her dream to go to Hollywood to be an actress. All she ever wanted was to become rich and famous. Her family didn't have much while she was growing up, so she imagined a life where she'd live in a mansion and drive a fancy car and wear fur coats. It was how she got through some bad times."

"She got the fur," Dawn mumbled under her breath, as Noel strode to the driver's side of the Jeep out of earshot. "Hat, that is."

The ride to the farmhouse was silent. She peered out the window into the dark wondering whether Noel was right. Was she overly sensitive? She tried to put herself in his shoes and imagine what it had been like to live with someone who had cried almost every day for months. It couldn't have been easy. That didn't mean, however, that he had the right to humiliate her.

He pulled into the drive and shut the car off. When she explained that she wanted to make up the bed with their own sheets, blankets and pillows, he pulled them out of the trunk and hauled them to the house. Then he made several more trips to carry in their luggage and the other odds and ends they'd packed into the Jeep.

Once their suitcases were in the bedroom and the front door was locked, he placed his hands on her arms. "I'm sorry about tonight. Will you forgive me and my big mouth? It was wrong for me to say anything to Maddie and Carl about your...our issues. You're right. Our business is nobody else's."

Dawn gazed into his eyes and saw the sparkle that had first attracted her. They'd fallen in love and married quickly, and their romance had been full of passion in the beginning. But the flame had sizzled, and they'd become more like roommates since she'd lost the babies. She really did want that feeling back again. "Of course, I forgive you." As she grazed her lips across his cheek, he moved his face quickly and pressed his lips to hers. The kiss was soft and sweet.

When they parted, he whispered, "That was nice. Should I go outside and see if there are logs for starting a fire?"

It would be romantic, but too much had happened today. Her nerves were on edge. She shook her head. "Maybe tomorrow night. I'm exhausted. Do you mind if we skip the fire and just go to sleep?"

He pursed his lips. It was evident that Noel struggled not to retort with something nasty. Without replying, he trudged up the stairs carrying the bundle of blankets, sheets, and pillows. She followed to find him unpacking some of his clothes and shoving them in the dresser drawers. Without speaking, she made up the bed.

After she washed her face and brushed her teeth, she slipped on a long-sleeved nightgown and climbed into bed. Noel seemed to be asleep already, based on his light snoring, so she switched off the bedside lamp and turned onto her side.

Her eyes drifted shut, and she realized the two of them were sleeping the same way they'd slept for the past few months, each of them on their side, close to their edge of the bed, facing opposite directions.

A lump formed in her throat and a solitary tear slipped down her cheek.

CHAPTER THREE

The next morning, Dawn woke to birdsong outside the bedroom window. She rubbed her eyes and glanced at the watch she'd forgotten to remove from her wrist. It was nine o'clock. Turning her head, she found the other side of the bed empty. No surprise there. Noel was an early riser.

The hardwood floor was cold when she slipped off the mattress and made her way across the room to the window. She pulled the drapes apart and saw two birds sitting on a branch of the oak tree, chirping. The sun was shining, too, a welcome sight after the rain and gloom of yesterday.

The house, however, was freezing. "It feels like an ice box in here," she chattered, folding her arms over her chest. She knelt and dug through her suitcase on the floor and found a chenille robe and slippers and felt a bit warmer as soon as she slipped them on.

The steps creaked as she went down them.

"Is that you, Dawn?" Noel's voice came from the little room he'd said was his pop's man cave.

She poked her head inside. His computer and monitor were sitting on the desk, and he was on the floor, dressed in jeans and a *Life is Good* long-sleeved

34

shirt, sorting out a tangle of cords. "Good morning," she said, attempting to sound cheerful. "Sorry I slept so late."

He turned his head. "I'm used to it."

Her smile dissolved. The comment stung, but she was determined not to let his remark bother her. It was a beautiful morning and a new day. Squaring her shoulders, she let the comment go. "I take it this is going to be your office."

"Yeah. It's going to be perfect if I can get the Wi-Fi to work."

"Wasn't that something you checked into before agreeing to work remotely?"

"Don't start," he said.

"I'm not starting anything. You'll be able to figure it out, won't you?"

"Of course I'll figure it out. I have to, or I won't have a job."

Alarm bells went off in her head. What if he'd moved them here without checking into the basics, like whether they could get Wi-Fi? Since she'd known him, Noel's nature leaned toward the impulsive. Putting their condo up for sale without consulting her was one example, and she could recall many more.

Anxiety pricked at her spine until she realized Noel was resourceful. And like most men, he did everything in his power to resolve any problem. There was one problem he hadn't been able to solve, however. That was her blue moods, as he'd called them. He'd begged her to get counseling after the second miscarriage, but she didn't have the tenacity or initiative at the time. After several hints, he finally stopped bringing it up. She was glad he'd quit bugging her about it, but unfortunately, they'd grown farther apart. He hadn't understood that all she needed was patience and empathy. As she expected, she'd started feeling better with time—without his help.

"Smells like coffee," she said, forcing negativity out of her head.

"I made a pot."

"Think I'll have a cup. Would you like one?"

He pointed to the mug on the desk. "Already have mine."

"Okay." She shivered, despite wearing the robe. The temperature felt several degrees colder downstairs. "Don't you think it's cold in here?" she inquired.

"Yes, I do, but I turned the thermostat down in the middle of the night because you woke me up saying you were sweating."

"I did?" She didn't recall waking up or talking to him. They'd had two blankets covering them when they went to bed, but they weren't extra thick. She hadn't felt sweaty or hot this morning. "I don't remember that. Are you sure I wasn't dreaming and talking in my sleep?"

"You jiggled my shoulder until I woke up. You looked me straight in the eyes and told me you were hot as blazes. You asked me to turn the thermostat down, so I did."

"Oh. Gosh, I'm sorry about that. I really don't remember. Anyway, it's plenty cold in here now."

"The thermostat's on the wall in the hallway if you want to adjust it."

"Yes, I'll do that."

She turned the temperature to 74 degrees and then stepped into the kitchen for the coffee. The room looked slightly less dreary in the daylight than it had yesterday afternoon, but nothing could make the old look new.

She filled a cup with coffee and realized there would be no cream in the refrigerator, nor any other food in the pantry. She wouldn't have wanted to eat any of it if there were, since it had been a couple of months since her in-laws had died.

When she strolled to Noel's office with the mug warming her palms, she asked him if he'd removed all the food from the house on one of his trips back.

"I cleaned everything out after the funeral. That's probably the first thing you should do is go to the market and stock up."

"Alone?"

"You saw the market on Main Street, didn't you?" He didn't look up, as he was busy plugging things into other things under the desk.

"Yes, but I thought we'd go together." Back in Chicago, Noel had taken over grocery shopping when she didn't have the energy to do it. Eventually, as she'd begun feeling more like herself again, they did the shopping together. The time together was something she'd come to enjoy.

"I've got to get my office set up so I can get back to work." He finally stopped his fiddling and gazed at her. "You don't mind going by yourself, do you? You won't have a panic attack or anything like that, will you?"

She squinted, never having once experienced a panic attack. "No, of course not. I'm sure I can find my way to town. It's not that big of a place, after all."

"Great. It'll do you good to get out on your own. In case you've forgotten, we live on Old Fort Road.

Just drive one mile down the road and then turn left onto Main Street."

"I remember the way. What about our boxes at the post office? When can we pick those up?"

"I was thinking we could hire someone with a truck to haul them here for us. It'll take several trips back and forth in the Jeep, if we don't."

"I'd like to get them as soon as possible. There are things in there I could use right away."

"The market has a board at the front door with names and numbers of people who hire out for odd jobs. Pick one and we'll call them when you get home."

"All right, if you're sure you don't think we can handle it ourselves."

"I don't have time."

Dawn left him to his labors and trod upstairs to take a quick bath. Once she was dressed and had applied makeup, she wrote out a list, then grabbed her purse and the car keys. By the time she popped her head into Noel's office to say goodbye, he was sitting at the desk watching something on YouTube. Seemed he'd gotten the internet to work.

"Well, I'll be going," she announced.

He craned his head over his shoulder. "Take your time and look around town. Thunder Point is small but charming. There's no time like the present to familiarize yourself with everything."

Shrugging, she replied, "Maybe another day. I'll get the groceries and be right home. I want to unpack our clothes, and if you can spare the time, I'd like your help in moving the rug out of the bedroom."

"What's wrong with the rug?" His gaze jerked from the computer and pierced her.

"It's really old and has a smell. I don't think vacuuming will revitalize it."

For a moment, he said nothing before replying, "Whatever you want. See you later. And don't forget to look for someone who will deliver the boxes to us."

"I won't forget. Oh, by the way. Could I have the house key? There must be a place in town where I can get a spare made."

He slipped the key out of his jeans pocket and tossed it to her before returning his focus to the computer screen.

There was a nip in the air, but because of the bright sunshine, it didn't feel as cold as the previous day. It was a perfect late autumn morning. The woods around the house didn't look as intimidating with sunlight streaming through the tree branches either.

She easily found her way to the Island Market and parked. As soon as she stepped inside, she was aware of people looking at her, some glancing, and some boldly gawking. Probably a stranger was someone to marvel at and be suspicious of on a small island where everyone knew everyone. *Maybe I should have worn a sign around my neck that said, I Am Noel Matheson's Wife.* Maybe then they'd figure out she was a local, even if by marriage.

One of the women staring at her stood at the produce table pretending to select tomatoes. She was older, probably in her fifties, with short brown hair. Wearing a plaid coat over jeans and work boots, she reminded Dawn of a female lumberjack. Dawn smiled and began to select lettuce and other salad fixings to place in her basket.

The woman returned her smile. "Hello. I haven't

seen you around. My name is Evie Rhinehart." She offered her hand to shake.

"I'm Dawn Matheson." She shook and noticed Evie had a shake as firm as a man's. For some reason, she felt compelled to explain herself. "You might know my husband, Noel. We just moved here from Chicago. We're living in his parents' house on Old Fort Road."

Evie's eyes lit up. "I'm pleased to meet you, Dawn. I can call you Dawn, can't I?"

"Certainly."

"I know Noel. Everyone in town was devastated by the loss of Betty, Tom, and Helen. Helen was the lady who hit them when she suffered a heart attack. Such a tragedy all around. I'm sorry for your loss."

"Thank you," Dawn said. There was no point in telling Evie that Betty and Tom had been her in-laws, but she'd never even met them.

"So, how do you like the old homestead?" Evie asked.

Dawn chuckled. "Well, I'm a city girl born and bred, so living in the country will take some getting used to."

"You'll adjust. How is Noel doing? I saw him at the funeral, but we didn't get a chance to talk."

"He's doing all right, considering."

"He and his brother got into a little spat at the cemetery and it nearly came to fisticuffs, so I was just curious. The chief of police had to break them up."

Fisticuffs? Noel had not mentioned getting into a fight with Keith. She didn't want to appear clueless, so she casually said, "Well, you know how brothers can be. Do you happen to know if Keith is still in Thunder Point?"

Evie shook her head. "Oh, no. I heard he skedaddled off the island on the ferry that same afternoon. Those two boys never did get along. Such a shame. With their folks gone, they only have each other now. Well, Noel has you, of course," she added.

"Keith isn't married?" Dawn asked.

Evie's eyes narrowed playfully. "You don't know?"

"I'm afraid Noel hasn't talked much about his brother," she admitted. For some reason, it seemed Evie could see right through her.

"I see." She looked around to make sure no one was eavesdropping and lowered her voice. "Well, Keith was married to a local girl by the name of Valerie Bauman for a couple of years. They recently divorced, and she lives with me now."

Dawn attempted to hide her shock. Was Evie admitting to being gay?

Obviously noticing her reaction, the woman laughed. "We're not a couple, if that's what you were wondering. Although, from the way I appear, I can see why you might think that. The truth is, I've been married three times and none of those men were worth a plug nickel, but that doesn't mean I've switched to the other team."

Dawn bit back a smile, and Evie went on without skipping a beat.

"I run an in-house program for women on my horse farm on Copper Falls Trail. Some have been victims of domestic abuse or have problems with drugs or alcohol. Some are homeless and need a place to stay until they can get back on their feet. They come to me with a wide range of issues. I have a master's

41

degree in counseling, and my job is to help them get their lives back on track. Since Thunder Point is small and we all know each other's business, most of my clients come from Big Bay across the lake, but there are a few locals who take advantage of my services." She glanced around again. "I shouldn't have mentioned Valerie to you, but her name just popped out of my mouth when you told me who you are."

Understanding that a breach of patient confidentiality could cost Evie her license and reputation, Dawn whispered, "I promise I won't tell. Your work must be very satisfying."

"It is. Do you work?"

"I did. I managed a large thrift store in Chicago. We specialized in selling name-brand clothing at bargain-basement prices. One of our goals was to provide homeless and unemployed men and women with a good-quality wardrobe as they were getting back into the work force."

Evie smiled, obviously pleased. "You were in the business of helping, too."

"Yes. I already miss the job and the people."

Evie high-fived her palm. "That was really great work you did."

Dawn smiled, feeling proud. The thought suddenly skittered through her brain that it could be a long time before she got another opportunity to be of service that way.

"Have you any leads on jobs here in Thunder Point?" Evie inquired, seeming to read her mind.

"No. We just arrived yesterday. We still have boxes to unpack and we need to get ourselves settled. That reminds me, my husband asked me to look on the board at the front door for someone with a pickup truck who can haul our boxes from the post office to the house."

"I know just the guy." Evie pulled a scrap of paper from the small backpack looped over her arm and wrote a name and number on it. She handed the paper to Dawn. "Call him. He'll take care of you for a fair price."

"Thank you. That's one thing off my list. Anyway, I'm not sure if I'm going to be working full-time again. Noel would like me to be home more." She felt weird confessing so much to a stranger, but Evie was so likeable and easy to talk to. She was probably a very good counselor. If Dawn didn't shut her mouth, she'd blurt out that she'd had two miscarriages, was afraid of getting pregnant again, and her sex life was all but dead and buried.

"Well, I'll leave you to your shopping," Evie said. "It was a pleasure to meet you." She turned to leave and then stopped. "Do you like horses, Dawn?"

Dawn angled her head. "I've never been around them. Why do you ask?"

"If you get bored sitting at home, come look me up. I don't have a budget for staff, but if you don't mind doing a little volunteer work, I could use someone at the barn a couple of hours a day, or whatever you can spare."

"The barn?"

"That's what I call my place. When I inherited Mom and Dad's farm ten years ago, I renovated the old horse barn. Half of it is became a house with three bedrooms, a kitchen, and a common room. The horses I use in therapy are stalled on the other side. You should come and visit. I included my address on that slip of paper."

Dawn felt a lump form in her throat. "Thank you, Evie. I would love to visit. I can't sit at home doing nothing for long, and I'd really like to do something to help people again."

"Because of privacy issues, you wouldn't be working with the women, but I sure could use someone to muck out the stalls, feed the horses, and that sort of thing."

Muck out stalls? The idea of working with horses was both captivating and scary. Those animals were big and intimidating.

Evie winked and pushed her cart past Dawn toward the check-out. She spoke over her shoulder. "Seriously think about it. I'm not just being nice. I really could use a helping hand."

"I definitely will. Thank you again."

As she strolled down each aisle tossing items into the cart, Dawn could barely concentrate on her grocery list for thinking of her conversation with her new acquaintance. What a coincidence that the first person she'd met who wasn't Noel's friend was so friendly and had offered her a job, or at least something worthwhile to do with her time. If horse wrangling didn't take her out of her comfort zone, nothing else would. She couldn't wait to get home and tell Noel. He'd be proud that she was considering the opportunity. Or, at least, she hoped he'd be.

As she paid for the groceries, she asked the teenage check-out clerk if he knew where she could have a key made. He told her there was a shop around the corner on Middle Road.

When she stepped into the lock and key store, it was empty of customers. The person at the counter said it would literally take one minute to make a copy of her key. Although the weather was cool, there was ice cream, milk, and other perishables in the car, so she was glad to be able to get it done quickly.

With a copy of the house key made, Dawn drove home feeling lighter than she had in a long time. That was, until she realized exactly what Evie had said. Keith's ex-wife currently lived at the barn, which meant…something, but what? Did his ex have emotional issues or a problem with drugs? Had Keith abused her?

She contemplated whether she should tell Noel what Evie said about Valerie. He might not agree on her volunteering at Evie's if he knew Keith's ex-wife was there. Dawn didn't know if it was only Keith that Noel didn't like, or his former sister-in-law, too.

It didn't take long for her to decide. She'd take her chances and tell Noel about Evie's offer. She'd already made up her mind that she wanted to volunteer. It might be exactly what she needed to integrate herself into the community. More importantly, it could be the thing to help get her passion about life back. She'd leave the information about Valerie out of it for now.

****

The moment she stepped through the front door, Dawn called out for Noel. He'd locked the door for some reason and didn't come to her pounding on it, so she'd had to put the sacks of groceries on the ground while she dug out the new house key and inserted it.

"Noel! Where are you? Can you help bring in the rest of the groceries?" She carried a couple of the bags in from the porch and stepped into the kitchen, where she set them on the table and began removing items. "Noel, did you hear me?"

"I heard you."

The sound of his voice made her jump. She hadn't heard him approach from behind. Whirling, her hand flew to her heart. "You frightened me. I didn't hear your footsteps. Could you bring in the rest of the bags, please?"

"Not yet." His mouth stretched into a tight line.

An odd sensation washed through her. "What's wrong? You have a strange look on your face. Has something happened?"

"Come with me." He grabbed her hand and led her upstairs to the bedroom where they'd slept. "Do you see something wrong in this room?"

She glanced around, but the room was still unfamiliar to her. "What do you mean by wrong?"

"Something belonging to my parents is missing."

"What?" Her gaze moved slowly around, having no idea as to what he was talking about.

When he pointed above the bed, she noticed. Where the painting of the cabin by the lake had hung, there was now a blank space. Faint shadows from having hung on the wall too long without dusting behind it were evident. "The picture is missing. Did it fall off the wall?"

His brow furrowed. "No. I looked behind the bed, under the bed, in the closet, and behind the drapes, and didn't find it."

Dawn was confused. "Where could it be? It was there last night when we went to sleep."

"Was it there this morning when you dressed?"

"I… I don't know. I suppose it was. I didn't pay attention."

His intense gaze caused her to back up a step. He took her by the arm and drew her into the hall. When he pushed open the door to what had been his brother's bedroom, he nudged her inside. The room was still decorated as if a high school boy lived in it. "Look under the bed," he said.

"What? Why?" Her eyes enlarged. The sharp tone of his voice startled her.

"Just look and tell me what you find."

Her heart began to thump. "What's wrong, Noel? I don't understand why you sound angry."

"Please, just look," he said.

"All right." She lowered to her knees and bent down. When she lifted the bed cover up and peered underneath, she gasped and let the cover fall.

"What do you see?" he asked.

"The painting. What's it doing in this room under Keith's bed?"

"I don't know. That's why I brought you in here, so you can explain. Why did you remove the painting from my parents' bedroom and hide it here? If you didn't want it in the room, you could have told me."

"I didn't remove the painting! Why would I?"

"I don't know, Dawn. That's the question I've been asking myself since I found it."

She ran a trembling hand through her curls. "I don't know what's going on, Noel, but I didn't touch that painting. I have no idea how it got in this room."

He sucked air through his nose, and it came out of his mouth in a whoosh. He helped her up from the floor and clamped his hands on her shoulders. "Maybe

47

you did it unconsciously and don't remember, like you don't remember waking me up last night and telling me to turn the temperature down."

"I didn't do that, either." Her voice sounded resolute, but inside, she wasn't as sure. Her emotions had been up and down like a roller coaster for so long. Depression changed brain cells, she'd read, and it caused people to behave in ways they wouldn't normally. "What reason would I have for taking the painting off the wall and hiding it? It's actually one of the few things in this house I like."

Noel shook his head, as if he were dealing with an insolent child. "There's no need to be rude. Our family didn't have a lot of money, like yours did, but Mom and Pop were happy and comfortable here."

Dawn worried her lip between her teeth. "I'm sorry. I didn't mean that the way it came out. It's just that you're accusing me of something I didn't—and wouldn't—do."

He guided her out the door and closed it behind them.

"Aren't you going to hang the painting back up over the bed?" she asked.

"No, if you don't like it, it can stay right where it is."

"I said I like it."

"That's enough, Dawn. I don't want to talk about it anymore. I think you should lie down and rest."

"I don't want to rest. I'm not tired, and I need to put the groceries away." She had been excited to tell him about meeting Evie, but now that was ruined. She hurried down the stairs and began unpacking the food. Blood rushed to her head, causing her to feel woozy. A moment later, the front door opened and heavy footsteps pounded across the porch and down the steps.

She peeked out the kitchen window. Outside, Noel slammed the trunk lid shut. His arms were full of bags as he approached the house. When he plodded into the kitchen carrying the last of the groceries, Dawn ignored him and continued putting the cold items in the fridge and freezer. What had gotten into him? She felt so angry and bewildered, the blood in her veins began to boil.

"I'm sorry, honey," he said, his voice quieter and contrite. From behind her, his cold hands touched her shoulders. "I don't mean to blame you. It's just that I don't understand how the painting ended up in Keith's room. I certainly didn't put it there, and there's no one else in the house."

Turning, she wriggled away from his touch and shouted, "Maybe it was the ghost of your mother!" Immediately, she felt bad for bringing his innocent mom into their argument. She apologized.

When he grabbed her and cradled her in his arms, tears spilled from her eyes.

"You've been under so much stress for such a long time," he said, softly. "And this move hasn't helped. I realize that now. But it'll get better, I promise. All you need is rest."

"I've been sleeping my life away for months," she whispered between sniffles. "I want to move on from the heartache. I want to feel normal again."

"It takes time," he said.

"No more time." She backed up and shook her head and wiped the tears from her eyes. "Something unexpected happened today. It's something I'm excited about. I wanted to tell you, but..."

"Tell me now," he insisted.

She described her conversation with Evie and the volunteer work she had offered.

Surprise lit Noel's eyes. "That's interesting, but you've never been around animals. Do you really think that's something you can handle?"

Why did he have to word everything in such a negative way? Had he always been so pessimistic? Or had love blinded her to his faults?

Ignoring the jab, she nodded. "Yes, trying something new would be good for me." She jutted her chin, using the phrase he'd so often repeated to her. "I want to feel useful. If you don't agree with letting me renovate this house right now, I have to do something with my time. I'm not someone who can sit in the house twiddling my thumbs all day. It seems like destiny that I met Evie today."

"I think it was, too."

Her eyes widened. "Then you're okay with me helping her? It's strictly volunteer work. No pay involved."

"It sounds like a plan, for the time being."

For the time being. It was clear what he meant, but there was no use in dissecting every little word out of his mouth. She threw her arms around his neck and kissed both of his cheeks. "Thank you, Noel. You'll see. I'm feeling better every day. It won't be long before I'm the confident woman I used to be. Soon, things will go back to the way they were between us."

A thin smile crossed his lips but didn't reach his eyes. "Whatever you say, Dawn. By the way, I locked the front door when you left, out of habit, the way we always did in Chicago. How did you get back in?"

Her head angled. "I had a spare key made while I was in town. I'd told you I wanted one."

"So you did." He stared intensely, as if he wanted to say more but refrained.

Her gaze followed him as he left the room. Within seconds, her good mood had dissolved. She sat at the table and placed her head in her hands, her heart plummeting. It was obvious. Noel didn't believe she hadn't removed the picture from the wall. Was it possible she'd removed it without remembering? If so, sleepwalking was the only logical answer, except she'd never been a sleepwalker before.

Taking several deep breaths, Dawn stood up and finished putting away the groceries. There was no use in working herself up. Strange as the incident was, she had more important things to do than try to figure out the impossible. First on the list was to call the person Evie had suggested for hauling. Needing something familiar to hold onto, she wanted her possessions in her hands as soon as possible.

CHAPTER FOUR

"I found someone who will load and unload our boxes for fifty dollars," Dawn told Noel later that afternoon. He was still in his office, but instead of working on his computer, he'd been scrolling, or maybe texting, on his phone. As soon as he heard her voice, he set the cell phone down on the desk and swiveled around in his chair to face her.

"Who?"

She referred to the name written on the sheet of paper Evie had given her. "Hal Nelson."

"Never heard of him."

She smiled. "Maybe you don't know all the residents of Thunder Point after all. He sounded fairly young on the phone, so maybe he's a teenager. Anyway, Evie gave me his number."

Noel shrugged. "Okay by me. Evie Rhinehart would be a good reference. When can he take care of it?"

"He can meet us at the post office right now. You want to go along to supervise the loading, don't you?" Noah was a perfectionist and didn't trust others to do what he felt he could do better. It was a wonder he'd agreed to let someone else handle their belongings at all.

"No, you can go, since you're so anxious. I'm still figuring out how I want to arrange my office." Mouth set in a grim line, he waited to see how she'd react. The thought suddenly crossed her mind that he was testing her. That, or else he really did think the change of scenery and lifestyle on Wolf Island would be good for her, and it was part of his plan to quickly force her into situations that had been uncomfortable in the recent past.

"Fine with me. See you when we get here." She made sure the house key was in her purse, pulled her down jacket from the hall tree, and tied a scarf around her neck. After grabbing her purse from the kitchen table, she said goodbye.

When she stepped inside the post office, Dawn was informed that Hal was already waiting in the back lot with his pickup. The clerk told her to drive behind the building to the loading dock, where she could make sure every box was accounted for.

A slim young man of around nineteen or twenty greeted her with a friendly grin and a firm handshake. He had a mop of curly dark hair and was dressed like most young people, in baggy jeans and a hooded sweatshirt. "Mrs. Matheson?"

"Yes, I'm Dawn. You must be Hal."

"Yes, ma'am. I'm Hal Nelson and that's my uncle. He's here to help." He nodded to a man leaning against an old blue Chevy truck with his arms folded across his chest. Dawn hadn't noticed him until now. He appeared to be around five-eight or five-nine and wore a baseball cap, a bomber jacket, and jeans.

"Austin Cooper," he said, tipping his cap and smiling. Blue eyes sparkled from a handsome, clean-shaven face.

"Pleased to meet you both," she said. "Thanks for meeting me so quickly today."

"No problem," Hal said. "Want to get started?"

"Sure."

Sitting on the loading dock was several stacks of boxes. As the two men lifted and carried them to the back of the pickup, Dawn checked to make sure her name was on each of them and that all the boxes they'd shipped were accounted for. When all fifteen were loaded, she breathed a sigh of relief.

"I was sure some of my things would get lost on their way here."

"You just moved to Wolf Island from Chicago, we're told." It was Austin who spoke.

"Yes. We arrived yesterday." It was a small town and she knew word had already gotten around. She guessed he was close to her and Noel's age. "Do you know my husband, Mr. Cooper?"

"Call me Austin," he replied, "and yes, I know Noel. He was a freshman when I was a senior in school, but we both played football. I remember watching him play for the junior varsity team. He only played that one year, but he was a good running back, as I recall. After I graduated, I still attended as many games as I could. Still do."

Did he say one year? The way Noel talked about sports, she'd assumed he'd played football all four years of high school. "What position did you play?" she asked Austin.

"Quarterback."

"Uncle Austin led the Howling Wolves to the championships two years in a row," Hal said, proudly.

"Very impressive. Where is the high school

located? I'd like to tour it sometime and see where Noel went to school. This is my first time to the island."

Hal spoke up. "Kids in Thunder Point go to junior and high school in Big Bay on the mainland. We only go through the fifth grade here."

"Oh. I had no idea." She chuckled, once again realizing just how much she didn't know about her husband's past. "I really have a lot to learn and see."

"I'm sorry for your loss," Austin said, changing the subject. "Betty and Tom Matheson were good people."

"Thank you." Again, she didn't bother to explain that she'd never met them.

"Betty was very sweet. Tom, he was respected, but I was told he was a tough nut." Austin shook his head and grinned. "But I guess Betty could handle him all right."

Dawn pondered on what his comment meant.

Austin continued. "Don't get me wrong. Tom was a good man, but he was a little rough on his boys, I remember."

"Rough?" A chill suddenly spiraled down her spine. "What do you mean?"

"Just that he didn't abide by slackers. The man worked like a mule and was a perfectionist. He held people to certain standards, and he expected his sons to exceed those standards."

That must be where Noel's uncompromising temperament comes from, Dawn thought. Funny, too, how Mr. Cooper had used the term perfectionist when describing Noel's father. The apple didn't fall far from the tree, apparently. "Do you also know Keith, Noel's brother?"

Austin nodded. "He was between me and Noel in school. I saw him at the funeral."

"To your knowledge, did he leave the island after the funeral? From what I know, he and Noel are on the outs right now."

Again, Austin nodded. "To my knowledge, he did leave. You weren't there, were you? At the funeral? I would have remembered."

"No, I wasn't able to come," she answered simply.

Hal cleared his throat. "We'd better get a move-on, Uncle Austin, if we want to get Mrs. Matheson's boxes unloaded before it storms."

The three of them peered into the sky. Sure enough, dark clouds were gathering and the temperature was dropping, causing Dawn's mood to dip. Winter was not her favorite season and it seemed to be quickly on its way to Wisconsin. "You can follow me out to the house," she said, walking to the Jeep. Of course, they probably knew exactly where the Matheson place was.

****

As soon as she pulled into the drive, Dawn stepped out of the Jeep and instructed Hal to back the pickup as close to the front door as possible, to make their job unloading easier. "I'll get my husband to help."

She jogged up the porch stairs and opened the front door and looked in Noel's office. Not finding him, she called his name. After perusing the empty house, she went outside and spoke to the men, who waited at the back of the truck.

"I thought Noel could help you unload, but he seems to have disappeared." She chuckled to hide the alarm bells sounding in her head. "We only have the one vehicle. I don't know where he would have gone on foot." She glanced around the property and toward the shed, but that door was closed tight.

"Maybe he took a walk in the woods," Austin suggested. "He could have gone to hunt for your supper." He and Hal shared a chuckle.

Distracted, Dawn said, "No, he doesn't hunt. Well, he used to, I think, but not anymore. Not since I've known him." But hadn't he said he might take it up again?

"We don't need his help anyway, Mrs. Matheson." Hal broke into her thoughts. "That's why Uncle Austin is here. He's as strong as an ox."

His uncle grinned. "I don't know about that, but I'll do my share. Let's get to work." He lifted the first heavy box out of the back of the pickup on his own, lending credence to his nephew's comment.

"I'll hold the door open for you." Dawn hurried up the stairs again and instructed them to stack all the boxes in the family room. Despite both men being in good shape, the two were huffing after hauling the fifteen heavy boxes up the porch stairs and into the house.

Once they completed the job, they stood in the foyer sharing small talk while catching their breath. Noel still hadn't shown up. Luckily, he'd left fifty dollars in cash on the kitchen table. It was a good thing, because Dawn didn't have but ten dollars in her purse and hadn't thought to ask Hal if he accepted a credit card. In Chicago, nearly every transaction was conducted with plastic.

"Thank you, Mrs. Matheson," he said, when she handed him the money. He immediately offered Austin half of it, but his uncle clapped him on the shoulder and shook his head.

"This business is yours, Hal. I'm happy to help when I can."

Dawn met his steady gaze and smiled, feeling her cheeks warm at his blatant stare. His charm and easygoing nature was attractive, and the kindness he showed toward his nephew was endearing.

"Can I get you each a glass of iced tea or water?" she asked.

"No thanks, I'm fine," Hal said.

"None for me either," Austin said. "We have bottled water inside the truck." Light rain began to fall and splashed against the hall windows. "Looks like we finished just in time."

"Guess we'd better get going, Uncle Austin," Hal said. "Thanks again, Mrs. Matheson. Give me a call if you have any other hauling to do or work done around the house. I'm a general handy man."

"I will definitely keep you in mind." She could think of a few things already, if Noel was too busy to do them.

Hal shot out the front door, leaving Austin standing in the hallway. He extended his hand to shake. When Dawn shook it, he held it a bit longer than she felt was appropriate, but for some reason, she didn't pull away.

"Don't worry about your husband," he said, finally letting his hand slip out of hers. "I'm sure he'll be home soon." Apparently, her face spoke of her concern.

She nodded and led him onto the porch. "It was nice to meet you."

"Same here. I expect we'll be seeing each other around town now and then." With that, he jogged down the stairs to climb into the passenger seat of Hal's truck, slamming the door just as the rain began to pour. Hal beeped the horn when they pulled out, and Dawn waved.

Her heart thudded inside her chest as she stood at the top of the stairs glancing around. Where was Noel? Why hadn't he left a note? He knew she hadn't planned to be long in town.

She moved to the far end of the porch and stared into the woods that grew darker as the rain fell heavier. The howl they'd heard yesterday skittered through her mind. If Noel was taking a walk and had come across that wild dog, if that's really what it had been, it could be rabid. He could have been bit, or he might have twisted an ankle falling into a hole or tripping over a downed branch.

In their three years together they'd never gone hiking or camping. He may have grown up doing those things here in the country, but he was a city boy now, and it had been years since he'd been so adventurous.

Just as she was beginning to think she should call the police for assistance, a car drove up the road and pulled into the drive. When Noel jumped out of the passenger side, a pound of pressure blew from Dawn's lungs. He waved to the driver and slammed the door and ran to the house. Because of the pouring rain, Dawn couldn't see who was driving.

"Where have you been?" she demanded, when he reached the top of the steps. Anxiety made her voice curt.

"When did you get home?" he said, sidestepping

her question and strolling through the door. In the foyer, he removed his damp jacket and hung it on the coat tree in the corner.

"Almost forty-five minutes ago. I've been worried. You didn't leave a note."

He slid a hand through his wet hair. "Yes, I did. Did you find the money I left on the kitchen table?"

"Yes."

"Well, the note was underneath the money."

"No. There was no note."

"Not again, Dawn." He sighed and quickly strode into the kitchen.

She stood in the hall and mumbled, "What do you mean not again?"

"Dawn, come here," he called from the kitchen.

Her stomach started to knot. When she entered the kitchen, he stood at the table holding a piece of paper in his hand. "What do you call this?"

She gently took the paper from his hand and examined the note. It was his writing. Scribbled quickly, it said he'd run out to help a friend and he would be back within the hour. Unease snuck along her chest wall. "Where did you find this?"

His finger stabbed the table top. "Right here where I left it."

Her head spun, replaying her movements since she'd gotten home. "There was no note there, Noel. I swear it. I found the fifty dollars to give to Hal, but that was all."

A low growl escaped his throat. "This paper didn't just appear out of thin air like magic, Dawn. Your memory is starting to slip. Why are you insisting it wasn't here when clearly it was?"

When she didn't answer, he slapped the paper on the table and walked out of the room and marched up the stairs.

Frozen like a statue, her breath released in a jagged shudder. What was happening? First, he claimed she'd asked for the temperature to be turned down in the house, and then he accused her of hiding the painting under the bed. Now this. Was she losing her mind, or was he messing with her on purpose?

"Noel, who were you with?" she asked, following his path upstairs and reversing the subject. He had removed his shirt and exchanged it for a dry one from his suitcase on the floor.

"I told you, a friend."

Her chest heaved with irritation. Why was he acting secretive? Coming here had turned her husband into someone she didn't recognize. "Who was the friend?"

He turned and smiled. "Are you jealous?"

"Depends. You haven't said whether your friend was a man or a woman."

Noel laughed and strode toward her and kissed her cheek. "You have nothing to fret about. My old buddy Scott heard I was back in town. He called and wanted to have a drink."

Scott? He'd never mentioned the name before. "You said you needed to help a friend."

"That's right. He's having a few issues with the wife and wanted to talk."

She narrowed her eyes. The only thing Noel and his friends in Chicago ever talked about was sports and politics. They avoided discussing anything of a personal nature like the plague, particularly relationship troubles.

"And were you able to counsel him to his satisfaction?" Dawn tried to keep the annoyance out of her voice, which was difficult. She felt the oddest sensation of having been betrayed in some way.

"I think I gave him a few good pointers." He swept past her and headed downstairs.

Feeling a flood of emotions bubbling inside, Dawn dropped onto the bed and pounded the mattress with her fists. When the flood gates opened, she plowed her face into her pillow and sobbed quietly. After a couple of minutes, she composed herself and went downstairs and robotically began unpacking boxes.

"Need some help with those?" Noel asked, entering the room.

"No thanks, I can do it." She turned her head so he wouldn't see her red eyes, but it was too late.

"Have you been crying?"

She didn't answer. He moved to her and turned her to face him. "I'm worried about you, Dawn. Where has your head been? I've never known you to be so forgetful, even in your darkest hours."

She closed her eyes and inhaled deeply. When she reopened them, she said, "A lot of changes have taken place in a short time. That's all. Don't make more of it than it is."

"But—"

"Please," she interjected. "I'm fine, really. The young man Evie referred to me delivered our boxes. I just want to get some of them unpacked before I start supper." And she didn't want to talk to him anymore. Even though it was unlikely, Dawn thought it remotely possible that she might have talked in her sleep and asked him to turn down the temperature. But in her heart, she knew she hadn't removed his parents' painting from the wall and hid it. Nor had she seen a note on the kitchen table.

Crying, combined with the hard rain pounding on the roof, had given her a headache, but she decided to let bygones be bygones and make Noel's favorite meal for supper: spinach stuffed ravioli. She'd picked up a fresh loaf of French bread at the market, as well as greens for a salad.

It had been a while since she'd cooked a proper meal. Even though the first two days on Wolf Island had not gone as she'd hoped or expected, it might lift both their spirits to share a nice meal and a couple of glasses of wine. She downed some Tylenol and began pulling ingredients out of the pantry.

Apparently, the scent of Italian herbs and spices drifting through the house was intoxicating. Noel snuck into the kitchen while she was putting the tray of garlic bread in the oven and wrapped his arms around her waist.

"You scared me," she said, jerking to a rigid stance. She accidentally let the oven door slam shut.

"Take it easy, Superwoman. That door might break off its hinges."

She checked his face for signs of irritation and found none. After a day of being exasperated with her, the smile she'd fallen in love with had thankfully returned.

"Smells delicious," he complimented.

"As soon as the bread crisps, we'll be ready. Would you like to pour the wine? I put a bottle in the fridge to chill, and I found our goblets in one of our boxes." She pointed to where she'd set two wine glasses on the counter.

"I'd be happy to."

Puzzled by his Jekyll and Hyde behavior, Dawn set the table with the salads and the hot pan of ravioli. As soon as the bread was done, she tossed the slices in a basket and placed it on the table. As her gaze moved over the nice spread, she realized something was missing. "I bought candles and a candle holder at the market," she remembered. After retrieving them from one of the grocery sacks still sitting on the floor, she lit a scented candle and placed it in the middle of the table.

"Very romantic," Noel said, holding out a chair for her.

She set and he scooted her in. Her body started to relax, grateful that whatever mood he'd been in for most of the day seemed to have vanished.

They held up their wine glasses to toast. "To a new and exciting life on Wolf Island," he said.

"To us," she added.

They clinked and sipped.

"Delicious," he said. "You chose a good one."

Before she could reply, a boom of thunder shook the house and the lights blinked on and off.

"The power might go out," he said. "I remember it happening all the time when I was growing up."

"What happens if it goes out?" She could imagine how spooky the house would be in total darkness with a thunderstorm crashing around them.

"Then we dine by candlelight."

"That would be romantic." She didn't know why she said it, because she didn't want to lead him on, but she did ache for some genuine romance. The moment the words tumbled out of her mouth, the lights flashed several more times and then went off altogether.

They stared at each other over the flickering candle.

"Did you plan that?" he asked, grinning.

She opened her mouth to answer, but the sound of a high-pitched cry caused her jaw to drop. It eerily echoed through the wind and rain. The hairs on her arms stood on end. "There's the wolf again!"

Noel smiled. "I told you, it can't be a wolf. No one has seen one on this island since before my grandfather's time. It's the wind."

"I don't think so." The next round of thunder boomed, making her jolt. "I'm not sure I'll be able to sleep if this storm keeps up."

Strangely, the lights flickered on just then.

"Well, that's a first," Noel said, gazing around the bright room. "Usually, when the power goes out in the country, it stays out for hours and sometimes days."

That was not something Dawn wanted to hear.

He dove into his ravioli like a man on a mission. After a few minutes, the rain stopped completely and the thunder rolled away, rumbling softly in the distance. "That storm didn't last long," he said, between bites.

Exhaling a gentle rush of air, Dawn dressed her salad and took a bite. When another lonely whine drifted into her ears, her gaze darted to Noel. "There it is again."

"What?" He didn't look up from his plate.

"The wolf. Don't tell me you didn't hear that."

"I didn't hear anything." He continued to eat without looking up.

Trouble settled on her once more. Either he really hadn't heard the howl, or for some reason, he didn't want her to know he'd heard it.

65

CHAPTER FIVE

Dawn didn't sleep well. Tossing and turning with nightmares of attacking wolves kept her awake most of the night. Apparently, she hadn't woken Noel, however, because he didn't mention anything when she went downstairs the next morning. He was sitting at the kitchen table with his hands wrapped around a coffee mug staring into space when she entered the room.

"Good morning," she said.

He jumped and turned his head. "I didn't hear you. Morning."

"You look deep in thought." She poured a cup of coffee from the pot and joined him at the table.

"Just thinking about Mom and Pop. I still can't believe they're gone."

She reached out, but he stood up before she could touch his hand. Feeling the brush-off like she'd been burned, she quietly said, "I wish I'd known them. We should have made more of an effort to visit. Three years and I never met my in-laws. It seems absurd."

He dumped the dregs from his mug into the sink. "Don't start that again, Dawn."

"I'm not starting anything. All I'm saying is that

it's a shame I didn't have a relationship with your parents or your brother. With my own parents gone, we don't have any family left between us, except for Keith."

"Keith left the island the day of the funeral, and good riddance to him."

"You're both grown men now. Surely you can bury the hatchet and forgive whatever issues there have been between you in the past."

"You don't know anything about it," Noel said, leaving the room.

She stood and followed him to his office, planting her hands against the door frame. She was tired of being dismissed. "Then tell me. I'm your wife. There shouldn't be secrets between us."

He plunked into his desk chair and tapped on the keyboard to wake up the computer. "I'm not keeping secrets. Keith is a jerk, plain and simple. We have nothing in common. We never got along, and we still don't. End of story."

Dawn suppressed a sigh. This was another battle she obviously would not win, at least not today.

"Are you going somewhere?" he asked, noticing that she was dressed.

She was dressed in jeans, a sweater, and her favorite leather ankle boots. "If you don't need the car this morning, I thought I'd drive to Evie's."

"So, you still want to help her with the horses?"

"Yes. I'll admit, the thought of handling large animals is a bit intimidating, but I'm also excited. You wanted me to become a part of my new community. This will be the first step. You're still okay with me helping her out, aren't you?"

He didn't hesitate. "Sure. I don't need the car this morning. I'm back to work now that I've got everything set up. Vacation time is over. The bills have to be paid." He smiled, but it was disingenuous.

Confused by the comment, Dawn said, "You've made it clear that you don't want me going back to work full time."

"We agreed living here would be better for you, what with the slow pace of life and all. I'd hardly call being a cowhand relaxing."

She tried to reply with the most playful tone she could muster, despite the twisting of her stomach. "Evie needs help with feeding and cleaning the stalls. That's all. No roping or riding involved."

He grumbled something incoherent and turned back to his computer. "I've got to get back to work. Have fun playing cowgirl."

Her temper sparked. "I will. And I'll stay out all day if that's what you'd prefer. I certainly wouldn't want to distract the breadwinner of the family since the bills have to be paid." Gritting her teeth, she didn't bother to return to the kitchen to finish her coffee. Practically since the moment they'd arrived at the house, Noel had acted differently towards her. It seemed she couldn't do or say anything right. Though it wasn't her usual nature to smart off, it felt good for a change.

For the next hour, she stayed out of his way. She did some unpacking and hauled the empty boxes outside, where she flattened them and shoved them into garbage cans. Physical activity turned out to be a great way to expend the angry energy that had built.

At 9:30, she decided it was not too early to head

to Evie's. She slipped on her coat and scarf, anxious to leave. Not intending to say goodbye, her hand was on the door knob when she heard the squeak of his chair and his footfalls.

"Hey," he said, filling up the office doorway. "How would you like to go see the underwater caves later? Remember, I told you about them."

Her tone was aloof when she answered. "I thought you're working all day."

"We can go early this evening. Are you up for a short hike?"

"How short and what kind of hike?" Although she'd played soccer in high school, the two of them had never done anything remotely athletic together since they'd been married, unless you counted fighting the mall crowds at Christmas time. It seemed moving back home had rekindled the outdoorsman in Noel.

"Thunder Point has a picturesque State Park with a trail to the caves that I'm sure you'll enjoy. In winter, people usually wear ice cleats because the walk is on sheer sheets of ice and the caves are frozen over. This time of year, it's a short hike across a mostly level boardwalk. We might have to cross over some dry riverbeds, but the view of the sun setting over the sandstone cliffs is tremendous."

"Sounds as if you've recently experienced the view."

"No, I have a good memory is all."

His roller coaster personality was starting to wear on her. "Can we wait to see how I feel once I get home from Evie's? She might put me straight to work today." Secretly, she was hoping so. After that last crying bout, she vowed to stop the waterworks. She was successful in her determination to get her life back on track, but it would be easy to lapse if she let Noel's surly attitude get to her.

His face dropped, and silence danced around them.

After a few beats, he spoke again. "I'm sorry about our little spiff earlier. That dig about paying the bills was out of line. I was stupid. Let me make it up to you by taking you on that hike. It'll be fun."

It had been so long since they'd done anything fun as a couple.

"Okay. It sounds like a good idea," she said, changing her mind. The last thing she wanted was another argument or the cold shoulder. Even if she came home dead tired from Evie's, she wouldn't let him know. Noel had sacrificed while she recovered from the miscarriages. He deserved more. "It's a date," she said.

"Great!" His eyes sparked with enthusiasm. "Be careful around those horses, and drive safe."

"I will."

Dawn referred to the directions Evie had provided and drove past the marina and turned onto Copper Falls Trail. The road meandered for two miles with woods on both sides before she finally reached what she thought must be the turnoff to the Rhinehart homestead. There was no sign to indicate that she was in the correct place, but it probably had to be that way due to the type of private facility Evie ran.

After another mile down a gravel road, she noticed horses in a fenced field near a red barn that looked like new construction. The property was more isolated than the Matheson farm. Dawn's hands clutched the steering wheel tighter, wondering if she'd done the right thing in coming. What had she been thinking? People she understood. She didn't know the first thing about caring for horses.

As she crept closer at a snail's pace, her gaze shifted to an old, more traditional looking clapboard house on the other side of the driveway. It was similar to the Matheson home, only without the double porches. Guessing this was Evie's dwelling, she parked in front of it and turned off the engine.

The curtains in one of the front windows parted and a face glanced out. The curtain dropped back into place. Before Dawn could change her mind and drive away, the front door opened and Evie stepped onto the stoop and waved.

"You can do this," Dawn whispered, grasping her purse and pushing open the car door.

"Dawn! Good to see you. Come on in," Evie hollered from the porch. She wore a similar outfit to the one she'd had on in the market, a flannel shirt over jeans and work boots.

"I hope I'm not stopping by at a bad time," Dawn said, reaching the stoop. The women shook hands.

"It's the perfect time." Evie flashed a toothy grin. "Come on in. I just made a pot of coffee. Would you like a cup?"

"I'd love one." Dawn shivered inside her coat. The temperature gauge in the Jeep had read 57 degrees outside.

The inside of Evie's house was as she imagined—no frills, simple furniture, not many decorations or pictures on the walls. Her kitchen was almost as outdated as the Matheson kitchen, except for a large center island with a granite top that set in the middle of the room with bar stools shoved underneath. Evie nodded for Dawn to take a seat at it.

"This is the house I grew up in," she explained. "It hasn't changed much since I was a kid, except for the addition of this kitchen island that I had installed. I like to bake and need room to make my messes." She chuckled. "When I inherited the property, all of my funds went into renovating the barn to serve two purposes. The front half is the guest house, and the back half contains the rebuilt horse stalls. I probably told you that already. I want the women who stay here to feel comfortable for as long as they're here. My horses need pampering as well. I don't need much for myself." She shrugged and poured coffee into a ceramic mug. "Do you take it black?"

"Cream, please."

"Will two percent milk do?"

"That'll be fine."

Evie pulled a carton of milk out of the fridge and handed it to Dawn to add herself. "I guess you saw the barn and the horses when you drove in."

"Yes. The barn is beautiful. How many horses do you own?"

"Six. My animals are certified therapy horses."

"I've heard about animals used for therapy, but don't know how it works."

"A few of the ways in which equine therapy helps is to clear an individual's blocked emotions. It helps the person better accomplish tasks and build personal confidence and self-esteem, discover intimacy and strength, reinforce relationships, and develop trust, patience, and responsibility. Primarily, horses give love where it's needed most."

"That's wonderful." Hope bloomed in Dawn's chest. She'd never believed in angels before, but she suddenly thought maybe an angel had guided her to Evie. Or Evie was her own guardian angel! Working with the horses might be just what she needed to rebuild her own confidence. Perhaps then, she and Noel could reconnect and become intimate again.

"Do you want to meet them?" Evie asked.

"I've love to."

They finished their coffee, put on their coats, and headed to the field. Upon their approach, all six horses trotted to the fence and nudged Evie's hand, which Dawn noticed held slices of apples that must have been stashed in her coat pockets. The animals were all different colors with thick fur and manes and tails that looked untangled and soft.

"They're spoiled." Evie gave each horse at least one piece of apple before handing Dawn a couple of slices. "Hold your palm out flat or they might bite your fingers."

A horse with a beautiful white mane slurped up the apple, leaving slobber on her hand. "That tickled." Not having a tissue in her coat to clean her hands with, she wiped them on her jeans, something she never would have done in Chicago.

"Did that feel good?" Evie asked, sliding her a sideways glance.

"Feeding the horse or wiping my hand on my clothes?"

"Both."

Dawn smiled. "Yes. Both felt good."

Evie glanced at her watch. "We have a group session starting in ten minutes. Are you ready to get to work?"

"Today? I wasn't sure if you'd need me yet, but I was anxious to see your place."

"I've needed you for the past couple of months. Follow me."

When they entered the back part of the barn where the stalls were located, Evie handed Dawn a pitchfork, a shovel, a scrub brush and a rake, then she wheeled a wheelbarrow from the corner. She stared at Dawn's expensive leather boots. "You'd better slip a pair of rubber boots over those, or they'll be ruined. There's a pair in the tack room over there. You'll find some work gloves in a box on the shelf, too." She pointed to a small room that she explained held horse gear, such as saddles, bridles, and a bunch of other stuff Dawn would never remember.

"Your main duty will be to muck out the stalls, but I don't expect you to do all of them on your first day. Start with one and we'll see how you do."

Dawn counted eight stalls altogether. "What does muck mean?"

Evie gave her a quick demonstration. "Clean stalls mean healthy horses. Roll the wheelbarrow as close to the stall door as possible, then use the pitchfork to sift through the bedding like this, and toss the manure and soiled shavings into the wheelbarrow." Evie forked some clumps of manure into the wheelbarrow. "Next, dig up the urine spots with the shovel. Geldings will usually urinate somewhere near the middle of the stall and mares will often pee near the back corners. Don't ask me why." She shrugged. "Once the stall is clean, you'll find a manure pile behind the barn for which to dump the waste, but if you're not up to pushing the wheelbarrow that far, leave it for me. Mucking can be back-breaking work, so take your time. Once you get used to it, it'll take about fifteen minutes per stall."

She pointed out the plastic bucket screwed into the inside wall of the stall. "Horses demand plentiful amounts of clean water. Each stall has an automatic waterer on the wall, but if the water looks dirty, you can scrub out the algae and any bits of hay with the scrub brush. Finally, put some clean bedding into the stall and rake it through so it mingles with the older bedding." Evie showed Dawn where the clean bedding was located. She looked at her watch again. "What do you think? Is that too much information for one day?"

Dawn shook her head. It did feel overwhelming, but she was willing to do her best.

"I'll come out and check on you as soon as group is over. Don't rush the work. Take your time so you don't hurt yourself."

"All right. Thanks, Evie."

The older woman winked and scurried out of the barn to disappear around the corner.

An hour and a half later, Dawn had mucked two stalls, dumped the waste out back, and was almost finished cleaning a third stall.

"Wow, I'm impressed!" Evie exclaimed, walking in and seeing what Dawn had accomplished. "Sorry that I'm a little later in returning than I expected. How do you feel? Does your back hurt?"

Dawn leaned against the pitchfork, feeling the strain. "Yes, a little, but it's the good kind of pain."

Evie laughed. "If you stick with it, your body will adjust. When you get home, take a couple of Tylenol or Advil, and take two each time before you come out. It'll help. A hot bath works nicely, too."

"I have a nice, deep tub at home. How often would you like me to come?" Dawn asked.

"I could use you every weekday morning for an hour or two, if it's not too much to ask. Whatever works for you is fine by me. I'm glad to have any and all help. I do have a teenage girl that comes after school when she can, but she's not dependable. Extracurricular school activities keep her pretty busy."

"I think I can manage every morning around this same time."

Evie took the pitchfork from her. "I'm grateful. You've done enough for one day. Go home and take it easy."

"I will, at least for a few hours." She stretched, feeling pain slice across her lower back. "Noel wants to take a hike this evening to the underwater caves and watch the sun go down over the cliffs. I hope I'll be able to walk."

Evie's forehead wrinkled. "Oh, gosh. You probably pushed yourself too hard."

Dawn waved her off. "No, I'll be okay. I'm out of shape. That's all. I haven't been very active for the past six months or so."

"I'll walk you to your car."

Dawn removed the rubber boots and returned them and the work gloves to the tack room and then limped to the Jeep. From the corner of her eye, she noticed three women standing at the fence petting the horses. The woman in the middle turned her head and stared. She was dressed in what seemed to be typical Wolf Island attire of jeans and a heavy jacket. She wore a knit cap, similar to Dawn's, over a head of long brown hair. She spoke to the other women and began walking toward Dawn and Evie.

"That's Valerie, Keith's ex-wife," Evie said. "I shouldn't even tell you that much, but she apparently saw you get out of your car when you drove up. Thunder Point is a small town, and word has gotten around that you and Noel have moved into the farmhouse. In group, she straight out asked me if you're Noel's wife. I didn't confirm or deny, of course, but she knew. I guess she wants to meet you."

Dawn felt her pulse speed up. "Technically, I guess we *were* sisters-in-law before she and Keith divorced, even though we never met."

Evie must have recognized Dawn's uneasiness. "You can get in the car and leave right now, if you want. You don't have to talk to her. There's no obligation on your part to meet her."

Dawn wanted so badly to know why Valerie was enrolled in Evie's program, but obviously, she couldn't ask. As Valerie approached, she flashed a tentative smile. "If it's not against your rules, I suppose it wouldn't hurt for us to meet," Dawn said.

Valerie held a gloved hand out the moment she stopped in front of the women. "I'm Valerie Bauman, and I'm guessing you're my brother-in-law's wife. I mean, former brother-in-law."

"Yes, I'm Dawn." She had her own gloves on by now and shook hands.

"Word in town is that you and Noel have moved into Tom and Betty's house."

"That's right." Dawn glanced at Evie, not knowing how much to disclose.

"Don't worry. Evie didn't tell me anything about you. She's the most trustworthy person I know."

"I wasn't worried. I sense that about Evie." Dawn

looked for signs of a weak and vulnerable person but found none in her first impression of Valerie. She spoke with confidence and made direct eye contact. "Noel keeps telling me how small the town is. I suppose we're the talk of it right now."

Valerie chuckled. "You can say that again. A lot of people have moved away from Thunder Point, but not many return, especially this time of year with winter nipping at our heels. I just thought we should meet since we were related by marriage until Keith and I divorced."

"I'm sorry," Dawn said, not knowing how else to reply.

"Don't be. The divorce was my idea."

"Well then, congratulations."

Valerie laughed out loud. "Thank you."

"I think we'd better let Dawn get going," Evie said, blowing hot breath on her bare hands.

"Sure. Sorry to keep you," Valerie said.

"No problem. It was nice to meet you."

"Same here." She hesitated a moment before saying, "Maybe we could have lunch together sometime. We're no longer sisters-in-law, but that shouldn't stop us from getting to know one another."

Again, Dawn subtly glanced at Evie for guidance. When she nodded slightly, Dawn said, "I'd like that." Apparently, Valerie wasn't dangerous and Evie saw nothing wrong with the two of them becoming acquainted. She looked forward to making another friend. Spending a little time with Valerie would also be a way to learn more about Keith and the issues that separated him and Noel. "When is good for you?"

"I'm free tomorrow around this time."

"I was planning on helping Evie with the horses again tomorrow. That is, if I'm able to get out of bed." She smiled, but it was the truth. Her back and legs had never had such a workout. Every muscle ached. "I would have to go home and change before we meet."

"Mucking stalls is the kind of physical work that takes some getting used to." Evie said. "Rest your body tomorrow. You can come back the following day."

"Are you sure?" Dawn was thankful that Evie had read her mind again.

"I'm sure."

"All right then." She spoke to Valerie again. "What time tomorrow should we meet, and where?"

"Do you like pizza?"

"Who doesn't?"

"Great. Let's meet at Tony's at noon."

Dawn smiled. "See you then."

"And I'll see you again in a couple of days," Evie said, as Dawn climbed into the Jeep.

"Yes, you will." She closed the door, started the engine, and waved goodbye.

When she turned onto Old Fort Road, her stomach began to roil. What would Noel say if she told him she'd met Valerie and planned on having lunch with her? Probably forbid her, which was why she wasn't going to tell him. She didn't like secrets, but if he wasn't going to offer information about his family, she'd have to get it somehow.

As she pulled in front of the house, she inhaled a deep breath and prayed that he was still in a good mood.

CHAPTER SIX

Noel greeted Dawn at the door, shocking her with a hug and a chaste kiss on the cheek. "How did your morning go?"

Her back was sore and her knees hurt, but she wouldn't let him know. It was strange how she wouldn't have hesitated to share her feelings with him before the miscarriages, but Noel had grown distant after the second one, and he'd changed even more drastically since they'd arrived on Wolf Island. He might suggest she don't go back to Evie's if she complained of pain. If she went straight up to bed for a quick nap, he would probably make another comment about her sleeping her life away. It was a phrase she'd heard too often in the past.

Dawn smiled. "It was great. You won't believe what your wife did."

"What?"

"I mucked out horse stalls and wheeled the manure to a compost pile outside, all by myself."

"Are you kidding?"

"No. And I got to meet Evie's horses and feed them apples from my hand." As she related her morning out loud, her spirit soared. The short time spent on Evie's farm had been so different from the Matheson place—the feeling was lighter and positive. "It was a lot of hard work, but it was also exhilarating. I like the horses. They didn't scare me one bit. Of course, they were on the other side the fence."

He smiled. "Didn't I tell you moving here would be good for you?"

"Yes, you did." She didn't like his haughty tone, as if she had a disease or a psychological problem and Wolf Island was the only cure. Hadn't the point of moving here been so that two of them could start fresh? Why did he always talk about her and the improvements she needed? His arrogance was insulting, but she was too tired to fight, so she let it go. "How was your morning? Did you get a lot of work done?"

"Yeah, but there's no rest for the weary, as they say. I still have a few more tasks to complete before we go on our hike."

She'd hoped he'd forgotten about the hike.

"You still want to go, don't you?" he asked.

"Sure I do. It sounds fun."

"Good." He seemed pleased.

"What time will we be leaving? I'd like to get the rest of the unpacking done today."

He glanced at his watch. "How about three o'clock? Will that give you enough time to do what you need to do?"

"Should be. It's already noon, so I can fix us a sandwich and soup first, if you're hungry."

"That would be nice. It's a sandwich and soup kind of day."

They sat at the kitchen table and shared small talk

while eating. It was pleasant. They laughed, reminisced, and he even complimented her on making the perfect sandwich. Then he stood up and placed their dishes in the sink. He approached the table and kissed her cheek again. It almost seemed like old times. "Thanks. That hit the spot." He rubbed his stomach.

"You're welcome." Her annoyance had worn off during lunch, deciding she'd been too hasty at judging him earlier. Maybe he'd truly meant his comment as sincere. Maybe she was the one needing a personality adjustment today.

When he playfully sniffed the air, she wondered why he hadn't mentioned the aroma of hay and manure wafting off her before now. "I'm going to take a hot bath and change my clothes before I finish unpacking."

"Take your time. There's no rush to unpack. I can help you tomorrow if you don't get it all done today."

"All right. Sounds like a plan."

As she ran water into the claw-foot tub, Dawn speculated at Noel's change in behavior and found herself humming with pleasure. This was the man she'd known when they first married—caring, kind, and sensitive. Maybe the stress of the move had temporarily altered his personality.

She stepped into the deep tub and slid under the water to soak. The heat felt terrific on her burning muscles. In no time, she became so relaxed that she fell asleep. When she woke 40 minutes later, the bath water was cold, so she quickly washed and stepped onto the soft rug and toweled off. Feeling refreshed and renewed, she looked forward to going to the caves with Noel.

As she changed clothes in the bedroom, her gaze went to the blank space above the bed. A blue chill briefly settled over her. Who had removed the painting and how had it ended up underneath Keith's bed? If it wasn't her and it wasn't Noel, a ghost must have done it.

She shook her head and rolled her eyes at the absurdity. Even if Noel claimed to feel his mother's spirit in the house, Dawn didn't. Ghosts did not exist. So, who was playing a joke on them?

There was no time to contemplate further. Noel called for her from downstairs.

"What is it?" she asked, finding him at the bottom of the stairs looking up.

"Did you fall asleep in the tub?"

"As a matter of fact, I did. I guess the work at Evie's was more tiring than I thought."

A frown appeared between his eyebrows. "You shouldn't overdo it. Maybe going out there isn't such a good idea after all."

She inhaled deeply and marched down the steps to stand nose-to-nose with him. "Noel, I'm not a porcelain doll that's going to break with a little hard work. You don't want me to get a paying job, but I won't be locked up in this house doing nothing. We have to compromise."

He jerked back like he'd been slapped. "No one's locking you up, Dawn. I'm just looking out for your wellbeing."

"I'm an adult and don't need you looking out for me." Her words bit, but she felt a rush of adrenaline race through her body, and it felt great. It had been a long time since she'd been passionate about anything.

She felt passion about living life on her own terms. "I'm sorry for snapping," she immediately apologized, "but I don't want to be treated with kid gloves. I'm doing so much better."

His gaze bore deep. "All right," he finally said. "Forgive me?"

She let out the breath she held. "Of course I forgive you. All I ask for is respect and understanding."

Out of the blue, he kissed her. It had been ages since they'd been intimate, and that included a passionate kiss. His mouth felt like a stranger's. Enjoying the moment, she didn't pull away, and the kiss grew deeper. Noel's arms went around her, drawing her close. Maybe, if they could start slow like this, it wouldn't be long before she'd feel comfortable enough to go farther. The thought was encouraging.

But when his hands suddenly grabbed her bottom and he ground his pelvis into hers, she broke the kiss and pushed away.

"What are you doing?"

"I thought you wanted to have sex."

"I really enjoyed the kiss, but kissing doesn't have to automatically lead to sex, Noel. I need you to be patient just a little longer."

His eyes flashed with fury. "I've been more patient than a saint. I'm not a monk, Dawn! How much longer do you expect me to wait? A man has needs."

Her heart began to beat fast.

Noel shoved a hand through his hair. "Maybe you don't want to be with me anymore. Is that it? Be honest."

That wasn't it—not entirely, but she remained

silent. He didn't understand her deep fear of getting pregnant again.

When she didn't speak, he stalked out of the room, leaving her alone. It seemed an eternity before he returned. When he did, he looked at his watch and his voice was composed. "It's almost two-thirty, and what work I have left to do can wait. I'm ready to go on that hike if you are. The fresh air will do us both good."

No longer in the mood to go anywhere with him, she also did not want to suffer his wrath again. Although he didn't apologize for blowing up, she did not want him throwing it in her face later if she broke her promise to go to the caves. Willing her accelerated pulse to return to a steady beat, she said, "All right. The boxes can wait, too."

They put on their cold weather gear. While Noel jogged out to start the Jeep, Dawn locked the front door.

He drove down Main Street and past the ferry landing and town gazebo to turn off onto a road where a sign stated that the Island Trail Head was six miles ahead.

When they arrived and he parked, Dawn saw that they were the only car in the lot. As soon as she stepped out of the Jeep, a hawk flew overhead. "Look at that." She pointed and then glanced around. "Wow, it's really pretty out here."

"And this is just the beginning of the trail. Let me put your purse in the trunk of the car. You won't need it, and it'll be safe there."

"Good idea. Thanks."

Once he'd slammed the lid down, they walked

across a long wooden bridge suspended over the river, where they spied a family of otters playing in the water.

"Look there!" Dawn pointed to a great blue heron with its wings stretched out sunning himself along the shore. "I wish we'd thought to bring a camera. It's packed away, I guess."

"Next time," Noel said.

At the end of the bridge, they stepped onto a plank boardwalk. At the sound of squawking, she gazed up to see a flock of herring gulls winging across the crisp blue sky.

"You don't see these kinds of shorebirds in Chicago," Noel stated.

Fifty yards off the trail was an observation deck.

"This is a great place to view wildlife," he said, taking her gloved hand. As soon as the words exited his mouth, a pair of whitetail deer emerged from a thicket. Their eyes darted in every direction, and then they pranced away to disappear as fast as they had appeared.

"Do you think we'll see a wolf?" Dawn asked.

He shook his head. "I told you, there aren't any wolves on the island anymore. But we might see a bear."

"A bear?" Her eyes enlarged.

He chuckled. "Just kidding. There aren't any bears on Wolf Island either, but they're abundant on some of the other uninhabited islands."

Once they got back on the trail, they walked along the edge of the peninsula through a hardwood forest fringed with fragrant pines. A chipmunk scurried along the forest floor, and a couple of squirrels chased each other up a tree. After a few easy stream crossings and a short, steep climb, a magnificent view of Lake Superior and the sea caves came into view.

"Oh, my gosh. Those caves are beautiful. I've never seen anything like them."

"Crashing waves and shifting ice carved the sandstone along the water line to form the caves," Noel explained. "In winter, hikers can take to the frozen surface of the lake to explore hanging icicles up close. Kayakers can explore them from the water on calm summer days." His eyes lit. "Let's take a look at the view from the cliffs."

Her heart leaped inside her chest. "Is it safe?"

"There's no ice yet. It's perfectly safe. I used to go up there all the time as a teenager." Before she could protest further, he grasped her by the hand and pulled her quickly across the hard rock surface toward a natural bridge that overlooked Lake Superior. From that height, and standing out in the open protected only by a couple of trees, the wind off the lake was much stronger than it had been on the ground. Dawn had forgotten to wear her hat, and she kept pushing fly-away hair back from her face.

Noel hollered, "Come on. Let's look down at the crashing waves below."

She shook her head. "I don't want to get too close to the edge. It looks dangerous."

"Don't be silly. The view is what we came to see."

"I can see just fine from here." She let her hand slip from his and backed up a few steps.

He hitched his shoulders in a slight shrug. "Suit

yourself." Fearlessly, he strode toward the edge of the cliff and peered over.

"Noel, don't!" Dawn uttered a sharp cry. If he started to slip, there would be nothing she could do to save him. "Please come back!" she yelled through cupped hands.

He smiled and waved her forward. "This view is to die for," he yelled back. He peered over again and then whirled. "I see a bald eagle's nest! And the mother is sitting on it. Come take a quick look. I don't want you to miss out!"

Her thudding heartbeats drummed erratically.

"Come on," he begged. The glimmer in his gaze nourished her confidence.

Wanting to prove something to Noel, she pulled in a breath and slowly walked toward his outstretched hand. The wind howled around her, cutting straight through her clothes. The sound of the waves crashing against rocks below caused her to feel a bit dizzy, but on she continued until her fingers grasped his.

"That's my girl." He wrenched her to his side and wrapped his arm around her. "Isn't it beautiful?"

Together they gazed upon the white-capped lake. Despite her mouth feeling as dry as sawdust, she managed to utter, "Where's the eagle's nest?"

"Down there." He pointed to the next cliff over.

"I don't see it."

"Move this way a bit." His arm dropped from her waist and his fingers prodded her back, pushing her closer to the edge.

"I still don't see a nest." Her neck was stretched as far as possible.

Suddenly, she felt her feet slip from underneath

her. Terror strummed her nerves as she felt herself tip forward. Sky and wind slapped at her face, and the sound of the waves pounding against the rocks boomed in her ears. Her mouth opened in a scream, but nothing came out. Spinning...spinning...there was nothing to hold onto—nothing to grasp.

I'm falling!

As quickly as she felt herself going over the edge, strong hands yanked her back. Pulled off her feet, Dawn flew backwards to land on top of Noel. Struggling to breathe, her heart gave a lurching thud. She could be at the bottom of the cliff dead right now.

"Oh, baby," Noel cried. From beneath her body, he held her tight and rocked her. When he finally rolled her over and pulled her to her feet, he grabbed her in a bear hug. Dawn felt his hot breath on her neck as his lips moved through her hair. "Are you all right, honey?"

When he set her back, she stared blankly into space. Her chest felt tight and sore, like she imagined it would feel after being thrown from one of Evie's horses.

Noel gripped her by the arm and snapped his fingers in front of her face as if to draw her out of a trance. "Dawn! Are you all right?"

"Yes," she finally mumbled. "What happened?"

"You slipped."

How had she slipped? She didn't even remember moving her feet.

"One moment you were looking for the eagle's nest and the next..." Noel's voice trailed off, apparently too shaken to continue. "Let's get away from here." He threw his arm around her and hustled her back to the main trail.

Their quick strides ate up the space between the cliffs and the lot where their Jeep was parked. They didn't speak until he'd settled her into the passenger's seat and started the car and cranked up the heat.

Shaking uncontrollably, in spite of warm air blowing from the vents, Dawn began to cry. The reality of what had just happened concaved her chest. "I could have died."

Noel leaned close and stroked her hair. "But you didn't."

Hot tears filled her eyes as she gazed into his face. "You saved my life!" Without thinking—only reacting—she grabbed his jaw between her hands. With a zealous look in his eyes, his mouth covered hers. Back at the house she'd told him she needed more time, but the near-death incident had her discombobulated. Wanting the physical assurance that she was indeed still alive, Dawn met his ardor as his lips swiftly became demanding. Breathless, he groaned, and she felt his desire heighten. In a wild frenzy, he twisted in the seat and unbuttoned her coat and stuck his hand under her shirt. As soon as he roughly tugged at her bra and squeezed her breast, she froze.

She broke the kiss and shoved his hand out from beneath her clothes. "Stop, Noel. We can't do this."

"Why not?" He tried to kiss her again, but she pushed him away and quickly re-buttoned her coat.

"Because we're in a public place and I'm not thinking straight. I almost died."

He took some deep, steadying breaths. "I'm sorry. More than you can imagine." Without another word, he buckled her into her seat belt, and then buckled his and silently drove them home.

Exhausted from the ordeal and Noel's erratic mood swings, Dawn waited until he popped the trunk and removed her purse from it. Then he opened her car door and helped her out, handing her the purse. The temperature had dropped significantly and the wind had picked up, causing her to feel even colder. All she wanted was to get into the house, make a cup of hot tea, and crawl under some blankets and try to forget that she'd almost died.

But that wasn't to be. As soon as they reached the porch, she screamed. Lying on the bottom step in a bloody mess was an animal of some kind. Before she averted her eyes, Dawn could see that its throat had been ripped out. She turned, and her hand covered her mouth. Bile crept into her throat causing her to gag.

"It's a dog," Noel said, with barely any emotion.

More tears sprang into her eyes. She couldn't bear to turn around and look again. If she did, she'd throw up. She faced the woods and closed her eyes, attempting to erase the horrible image from her mind. "What do you think happened to it?"

"I guess another animal attacked it."

"What kind of animal could have done that?"

"I don't know. Another dog, I suppose."

She craned her head over her shoulder. Noel was kneeling beside the step. "Don't touch it!" she shouted.

"I'm not," he snapped. He abruptly stood. "Let's get into the house before you have a major meltdown."

"What are you going to do with the animal?"

"Dispose of it." He took her arm and ushered her around the carcass and up the steps to the front door.

"Shouldn't we call the police or the animal control center?"

"There's no animal control on the island. Besides, what would be the purpose? This was clearly an act of nature."

She quickly glanced at the poor animal again. "But don't you think it's strange the way it's laying on the bottom step?" Logic kicked in. "I doubt it crawled up there and died. If two animals had a fight in the yard, it would have died in the yard. It wouldn't have been able to crawl up onto the step. If they'd fought on the steps, there would be blood everywhere." A shiver racked her body. "I wonder if someone placed the animal on the step to scare us."

Noel winced. "Why on earth would someone do that, and who would do such a thing? We don't have any enemies. You're talking crazy, Dawn."

The retort stung. "I'm not crazy, Noel. I'm simply thinking of all possibilities."

He shrugged. "If you want to call the police, go ahead. I don't care one way or the other."

Obviously, he was hurt from her rejection in the car. He hadn't spoken all the way home, but she didn't care. He'd taken advantage of her while in an extremely emotional state.

At the door, he gruffly said, "Give me your house key."

She dug into her purse and found her keychain, but the new house key wasn't on it. He sighed and waited as she continued to dig.

"I know the key was on this chain." She fumbled through everything once more and then dumped the contents of the purse out onto the porch floor.

"Don't tell me you've lost it, Dawn." Noel's fists planted on his hips, and he sighed heavily.

"I didn't lose it," she insisted. "I had it when we left. I even locked the front door with it."

For some reason, he turned the knob. The door opened. He grunted. "You locked the front door, did you? Doesn't look like it to me. And now you've lost your key. Honestly, I don't know where your brain is these days." Without helping her pick up the contents of her purse, he stepped inside the house.

Her nerves rippled beneath her skin. "I didn't lose it," she mumbled, as she stuffed everything back into her purse and entered the house. She replayed her steps in her mind and was pretty sure she'd locked the door when they left. Unfortunately, she'd been distracted by his bad disposition—once again. Maybe she *had* forgotten to lock it, as Noel suggested. At any rate, she needed to find the key, but first things first.

"Are you going to call the police?" she asked, entering his office and noticing he'd tossed his coat on the recliner. He was standing in front of the gun rack staring at the weapons.

"You call them if it's that important to you." He briefly met her gaze, then he sat at his desk and roused the computer from sleep mode.

He was angry, but someone had to do something about the dead animal. It seemed Noel wasn't even going to remove it from the step, as he'd said. She went into the family room and called the police station from her cell phone. The dispatcher said someone would be out shortly.

Within fifteen minutes, Dawn heard a vehicle pull into the drive. When a knock sounded on the door, she went to it, seeing that Noel wasn't going to answer it. She soothed her expression into a calm mask and opened the door.

A man in jeans and a bomber jacket tipped his head in greeting. When he removed the aviator sunglasses from his eyes, her mouth dropped open.

"Hello, Mrs. Matheson. Nice to see you again, although I'm sorry it's under these circumstances." He cocked his thumb over his shoulder, referring to the animal on the bottom step.

Her anxiety ebbed into calm at his warm smile and soothing voice. "Hello, Mr. Cooper. What are you doing here?"

"You telephoned. I'm the Chief of Police, but please, call me Austin."

CHAPTER SEVEN

"I had no idea," she said. "You didn't mention your occupation when we met."

"I was off duty at the time. Figured you'd find out eventually. Sorry it had to be this way though. When did you discover the animal?"

At the sound of his voice, Noel stepped into the hall and nodded. "Austin."

"Noel." Austin offered his hand to shake.

Dawn stepped aside and motioned for him to enter. "Please come inside, where it's warm and it'll be more comfortable to talk."

"Thank you." Once he stood in the foyer, he asked a few questions to establish a time line.

"I told her there was no need to bother the police," Noel said, frowning at Dawn. "This was a dog fight, pure and simple."

"I don't think so," Austin said.

"What do you mean?"

"Is the animal a wolf?" Dawn asked, feeling her nerves zing with anticipation.

"No, it's a dog," Austin answered, "but it appears to have been attacked by something other than another dog."

"Such as a wolf?" she pressed.

"Don't be ridiculous." Noel's voice was laced with irritation.

Austin's steady gaze shifted between the couple. "It's not so ridiculous. The wounds to the throat do resemble those of a wolf attack, although I don't know how to explain it since there have been no wolf sightings in decades."

Feeling exonerated, Dawn locked eyes with her husband. She allowed the hint of a smile to curve her lips.

Obviously frustrated, Noel changed the subject abruptly. "Can you dispose of the carcass for us, Chief?"

"Be glad to, but keep a lookout for wild animals coming out of the woods. You don't want to mess around with rabid animals. Do you have a shotgun for handling that sort of thing, Noel?"

"My dad's guns are in good working order, and I know how to use them."

"Good." Austin's gazed moved to Dawn. "What about you, Mrs. Matheson? Do you know how to shoot?"

She shook her head, not wanting to hold a gun let alone shoot one.

"It might be a good idea if you give her a few lessons," he told Noel. "A woman living this far out should know how to protect herself."

"I'll protect my wife, Chief Cooper." Noel didn't smile. He opened the door and clapped Austin on the shoulder to end the conversation. "Sorry to have troubled you, but thanks for hauling away the animal."

When Austin's empathetic gaze landed on Dawn,

a trace of acknowledgment passed between them. Unexpected stirrings made her look away; her gaze fell to the ground. She hadn't felt the arousal of desire for months. What she felt now wasn't sexual, but considering the strain between her and Noel that had almost reached a boiling point, it was no wonder she was susceptible to the police chief's warm smile and kindness.

Austin tipped his cap. "Good day, Mrs. Matheson. Keep a watch out, like I said."

She met his gaze again and spoke softly while feeling heat rise in her cheeks. "I will. Thank you for coming out and taking care of—"

"You're welcome," he interjected. "Call me if you need anything at all."

Noel practically shoved the man out the door. "We will." He closed the door and stepped into his office, officially wiping his hands of the mess.

Dawn entered the kitchen and peeked out the window to watch Austin don gloves and a shovel from the back of his police truck. With quick work, he extracted the nearly decapitated dog from the front steps. Her gaze stayed glued as he carried it to the back of the truck. She was still staring through the parted curtain when he strode to the passenger side of the vehicle and flung open the door.

As if he sensed her, he looked up and their gazes met. The corner of his mouth lifted in a smile. Letting the curtain drop, she stepped away from the window and pressed her back against the wall. While listening to the sound of his tires crunch over the gravel driveway and move down the road, guilt stabbed at her like a sharp pinch.

She loved Noel, but their relationship had changed so drastically. She barely recognized him anymore. Could they ever return to what they'd had as newlyweds? If she did get pregnant again, maybe the third time would be the charm. But what if she lost another baby? Or their relationship continued to steadily disintegrate? The distance between them was growing wider apart with each put down and accusation.

She tiptoed into the hallway and quietly stood outside of his office. Glancing around the door frame, she saw him scrolling down the screen of his cell phone with a finger. When he swiveled halfway around in his chair, the dazzling grin that filled his face caused her to quietly gasp.

Curiosity sparked like kindling inside her.

It had been so long since he'd graced her with that brilliant smile. What, or who, had brought it out in him?

For the first time in their marriage, Dawn seriously wondered if she could trust her husband.

****

The next day, she dressed as if she was going to Evie's, so Noel wouldn't ask questions. If she told him she was meeting a friend for lunch, he'd ask who she was meeting, since she didn't know anyone in town. She didn't want to lie.

"See you this afternoon," she said, breezing past his office and out the door. If he replied, she didn't hear him, because she quickly climbed into the Jeep and drove away.

Arriving in town early, Dawn browsed through

the shops, though her mind was not on shopping. When she finally entered Tony's pizza parlor, Valerie was already sitting at a table in the corner and waved her over.

"Glad you could make it," she said in greeting.

Dawn slipped out of her coat and hung it on the back of the chair and sat. "Thanks for the invitation."

After the server brought water and menus, Valerie said, "I'm surprised Noel allowed you to come, knowing you were going to meet me. He and I never saw eye-to-eye."

"I didn't exactly tell him," Dawn admitted. "To be honest, he hasn't told me much about his brother or his parents, and nothing about you."

Valerie flashed a knowing smile. "Is that why you came today, to needle me about the Matheson family?"

Feeling like a kid caught with her hand in the candy jar, Dawn replied, "Am I that easy to read?"

Valerie chuckled, but seemed not to be insulted. "No, but if I were in your shoes, I'd do the same thing if given the opportunity. In fact, when I heard Noel had brought a woman—his bride—to the island, I wanted to meet you, even though I'm no longer part of the family. It was such a surprise."

Dawn tilted her head. "Why is that?" She immediately liked the no-nonsense Valerie.

Before she could answer, the server returned. Once their orders were taken, Valerie responded. "Well, we had no idea Noel had married. You didn't invite any of us to the wedding, and as far as I knew, you never called or corresponded with Betty and Tom. Am I wrong in my assumption?"

Dawn's mind whirled. "I don't understand. I sent

all of you wedding invitations. Noel told me his parents were too elderly to travel, and he said he and his brother didn't get along, so he doubted Keith would attend."

"Elderly? Tom was sixty-one and Betty was sixty when they passed. I'd hardly call that decrepit. They were in pretty good health."

Frowning with that bit of news, Dawn continued. "Later, when I suggested more than once that we come to the island for a visit, there was always a reason why we couldn't. And I did send letters as well as a Christmas box to Mr. and Mrs. Matheson the first year we were married. It hurt that they didn't respond, not even with a thank you note, but Noel asked me to understand. He said they were a little backwards and not well versed in proper etiquette."

"Backwards?" Valerie's eyebrows winged downward. "What did he mean by that?"

Dawn felt her cheeks warm, embarrassed by having used that term. "I suppose he meant that they were private people who kept to themselves. He told me his mother wasn't much of a letter writer. To be honest, I thought his parents simply had no interest in meeting me, let alone communicating with me, and I didn't understand why. After three years of marriage, I gave up trying to get information out of Noel." She'd also been dealing with the miscarriages and depression and couldn't worry about anything else at the time, but Valerie didn't need to know those details.

Valerie placed her hand on top of Dawn's across the table. "I'm sorry, but I was married to Keith for five years before we broke up a few months ago, and we spent a lot of time with Betty and Tom. They never received any letters or Christmas boxes from you that I'm aware of. And Noel sure as hell never told them he'd gotten married."

Dawn considered Valerie's comment for several long moments. Under the table, her hands shook. Her next words came out in a whisper. "Obviously, Noel lied to me. He never told his family about our marriage, and he must have intercepted the mail." She felt her throat begin to tighten. "Why would he do such a thing?"

Valerie had no answers, but her gaze showed empathy.

The server brought their lunch, and though Dawn nibbled at her slice of pizza and salad to be polite, it was difficult to concentrate on anything except Noel's betrayal.

"You're probably wondering why I'm staying at Evie's," Valerie said, changing the subject.

That snapped Dawn out of her puzzled stupor. "It's none of my business."

"True, but I want to tell you, so you don't get the wrong idea about me."

"All right. I'm listening."

"The truth is I have nowhere else to go. When I filed for divorce, Keith made life tough for me at first, because he was upset and angry that I wasn't willing to give him another chance. I even thought he tried to get me fired from my job, but I later found out that wasn't the case. I got pneumonia right in the middle of the whole mess and ended up losing my job anyway. There wasn't much left in our bank account when we divorced, and I'm a prideful woman and wasn't going to ask Keith for money. He left the island, and I had little to nothing. That's it in a nutshell. Evie has been kind enough to give me a place to live while I try to get back on my feet."

"I'm sorry to hear of your struggles," Dawn said. "Was Keith ever…"

"Abusive?" Valerie broke in. "He does have a temper, like all the Matheson men, but he never hit me. Yes, there were a couple of incidents in the past where we had been drinking and neighbors called the cops, but we were both at fault. With Evie's help, I'm learning how to resolve conflict without screaming and throwing things. I'm also thirty days sober." She offered a weak smile.

Now it was Dawn's turn to pat Valerie's hand in sympathy. She liked her and wouldn't judge her, especially now that she'd discovered that Noel had made her look like a fool and worse, lied to her. "Congratulations on the thirty days. That's a great accomplishment."

Valerie continued. "Keith isn't completely to blame for our marriage falling apart. My own parents weren't role models when it came to love and devotion. I attend both group and one-on-one sessions with Evie. It's been enlightening to figure out why I've made some of the decisions I have in my life. Every day I'm getting healthier in mind, body, and spirit. I particularly like working with the horses. They help me focus on something other than myself. Evie and those beautiful creatures have been my life savers."

Smiling, Dawn forgot her own troubles for a moment. "Valerie, we just met, but I'm very glad to hear you're doing well, and I hope we can get together again soon. We might not be related by marriage any longer, but I'd like it if we could be friends. I left everyone close to me behind in Chicago, so I could use a friend here on Wolf Island."

"I'd like that, too. A person can never have enough friends. Are you going to confront Noel about his lies?"

"I don't know. I'm very confused right now and need some time to think."

"Don't hesitate to give me a call if you want to talk more." She scratched her cell phone number on a piece of paper and handed it to Dawn.

"Thank you." Dawn stuffed the paper into her purse. When the bill was paid, she stood up and slipped on her coat.

As the two women were parting company outside the pizza place, a familiar looking blonde woman approached the door. She glanced between Dawn and Valerie and then nodded hello. Dawn nodded, too, out of politeness, and the blonde entered the restaurant.

"Do you know that woman?" Dawn asked Valerie.

"Can't say that I do."

"She looks so familiar, but I've only met a few people here. Oh, well. Goodbye. Maybe I'll see you tomorrow when I come out to Evie's."

Valerie clasped her hand. "Take care, and good luck, if you decide to talk to Noel."

When Dawn got into the Jeep, she suddenly remembered where she'd seen the blonde woman. Valerie mentioning Noel had triggered the memory. The blonde was the woman who'd been standing with Madeline Reed at the gazebo on the day they arrived.

She was another high school friend of Noel's. Leslie, he'd said her name was.

Dawn drove the road home as slowly as possible to allow herself time to think. Why had Noel kept their marriage secret from his parents? Why had he intercepted her correspondence with them? It made no sense, and his actions didn't correlate to the man she'd married—or thought she'd married.

CHAPTER EIGHT

"You don't smell like horse crap today." It was not the greeting Dawn expected when she entered the house.

She shucked off her coat. As much as she wanted to confront Noel about his lies, his antagonistic attitude was off-putting. It wasn't the right time.

"Good afternoon to you, too," she replied, emotionless. "Evie asked me to clean the tack room today," she fibbed. "There's no manure to muck in a tack room. If you'll excuse me, I have a headache." She set her purse on the hall bench and went upstairs for the bottle of pain reliever located in the bathroom medicine cabinet. Not wanting to speak or even look at Noel, she called from the top of the stairs, "I'm going to lay down for a short nap."

He popped out of his office and stood at the bottom of the staircase with his arms crossed over his chest. "Before you do, there's something I want to ask you."

"What's that?" She desperately tried to keep the sigh out of her voice.

He held up a shiny metal key. "Do you recognize this?"

"Is it my house key?"

"Apparently."

She slowly made her way down the stairs to stand in front of him. "Where did you find it?"

His face hinted of displeasure. "In the cupboard in the coffee can, which is full of coffee grounds."

Her head angled, and she would have laughed if their relationship weren't so strained. "That doesn't make any sense. You're joking, right?"

"I'm not joking, and no, it doesn't make sense. Why on earth would you hide your house key in a can of coffee?"

"I didn't." She snatched the key out of his hand, feeling her temperature rise.

"Really, Dawn, I'm very worried about you." When he reached out to place his hands on her arms, she abruptly turned and marched up the stairs. "Something's not right," he said. "It's been one thing after another since we got here. Maybe you should see a doctor and get a prescription."

Something was not right, for sure. Without replying, she huffed and shoved the key in her jeans pocket.

"You know," Noel called from below, "I've been doing a lot of reflecting and don't think it's a good idea for you to get pregnant anytime soon. Maybe never."

She stopped at the top of the stairs and whirled, not believing her ears. "What? Are you saying you don't want a child anymore?"

His intense stare didn't waver. "Yes, that's what I'm saying."

"Are you kidding? You're the one who's been harping on having a baby."

"Harping? Really, Dawn. I thought you wanted a child, too."

"I did…"

"Anyway," he interrupted, "I don't think it would be responsible of us to bring a child into our lives. Not with your… issues."

"My issues?" It was nearly impossible for her to keep from screaming.

"Your mental instability," he clarified, attempting to sound sincere. "It's clear that the miscarriages, the depression, and now the move and upheaval of your life has caused you more stress than you can handle."

"It was your idea to move here," she snapped.

He nodded. "I acknowledge that and I'm sorry, but I can't bring a child into the world under these conditions."

Dawn felt a strange mixture of relief and hurt at being deceived. Baby or no baby, now more than ever, she needed to know the truth as to why he'd lied to her and his family. "Seems I have no say in the matter, just as I didn't have a say in attending your parents' funeral or uprooting our lives and leaving Chicago." She inhaled deeply. "There's something you need to know."

"What's that?"

"I didn't go to Evie's today."

"Oh? Then where have you been for the last couple of hours?"

The flicker in his eyes gave her the oddest feeling that he already knew. "I had lunch with Valerie Bauman, your sister-in-law."

"My former sister-in-law," he corrected. "I had no idea you knew her." Surprisingly, his tone was flat,

107

but she did notice his fists clasping and unclasping at his sides.

"I met her yesterday. She'd heard we'd moved here and asked if I wanted to have lunch. I said yes."

"Why?"

"Technically, she was my sister-in-law, too, even though we never had the chance to develop a relationship. Turns out that was entirely your fault, and I want to know why." She suddenly felt in control of her emotions and as powerful as a Midwestern tornado. From the twist in Noel's face, he understood that his secrets were about to be blown wide open. "Valerie enlightened me on the truth, Noel. How you never even told your parents, or Keith and Valerie, about our marriage. How you must have intercepted the letters and Christmas packages I sent to your family. How you lied to all of us. For the life of me, I don't understand. Why'd you do it?"

For a fleeting moment, Dawn feared he might strike her. His face grew red and his eyes burned with fury. After a few long beats, his voice dropped low and was weirdly in control when he replied, "You don't know what you're talking about, Dawn."

"Then by all means, fill me in."

"All right, I will. Valerie's a liar, as well as an alcoholic. Why do you think Keith divorced her and she's getting treatment at Evie's place?"

That he knew *that* information stunned her, but she wouldn't react. "What makes you think she's being treated by Evie?"

"This is a small community, Dawn. These are my people, and I have a way of finding out things. Don't forget that."

"That sounds like a threat, Noel." Somehow, she managed to sound calm, but inside her stomach grew queasy.

He sighed and slicked a hand through his hair. "Sorry. It wasn't intended that way. I'm just saying you don't know anything about Val. She's not to be trusted."

"Valerie claims you're the one I can't trust, and I tend to believe her, after what I heard today."

"Oh, for God's sakes, Dawn. Val is mental. I saw her behavior firsthand."

"And now you believe I'm mental, too. By the way, Keith didn't divorce Valerie; she divorced him."

"What's the difference? They both have issues. Who are you going to believe, a woman you just met or your husband?"

"Do you really want me to answer that, Noel? After all you've accused me of, and now, after I find out you kept me hidden from your family on purpose?" When he didn't reply, she continued. "What possible reason did you have for not wanting me and your parents to know each other? I begged so many times for you to bring me here to meet them. You always had an excuse. Like an idiot, I let you get away with it. When I found out today that they never knew I existed, I was shocked beyond belief. I still am."

He shook his head. "There's nothing I can say that will make you understand."

"Try!"

He turned and stomped to his office. "You've already pegged me as a liar. What's the use?" He slammed the office door, leaving her staring after him, unbelieving. How had her marriage disintegrated so quickly and thoroughly?

She ran up the stairs with her own fists clenched at her sides. After slamming the bedroom door, she turned the lock and flung herself onto the bed, throwing her arm over her face. Tears stung her eyes, but she held them in this time. Instead of crying, she turned onto her stomach and punched the pillow, imagining it was Noel. It felt terrific to release her anger. Over and over she pounded the pillow into oblivion.

Before long, she gave in to emotional exhaustion and fell asleep. When she woke up and went downstairs to peek out the front door, the sun was setting and gloom was quickly settling over the yard. It looked like it could snow. Realizing the house was quiet and Noel wasn't in his office, she did a quick search of the first floor. No Noel. No note either, but his coat was missing from the hall coat tree. The Jeep, however, was still parked outside.

Dawn inhaled. Good. Maybe he'd taken a walk. She wasn't up to facing him after that last ridiculous accusation that had led to opening up the can of worms. The longer he stayed away the better. There was no way she'd hide a key in a coffee can! And he refused to tell her the truth as to why he'd kept her a secret from his family. Was he *trying* to drive her crazy?

Before she could contemplate further, the distinct sound of a high-pitched howl cut through her thoughts. Wolf! Throwing open the front door, she ran to the end of the porch to visually search the woods. The howling immediately stopped. Not moving a muscle, she waited and watched. The woods darkened with each passing second. As she continued to peruse the area, another sound drifted out from amongst the trees. A low whine at first, it quickly revved to a full-blown baby's cry.

Dawn hugged herself as a sudden wind chilled her and blew curls around her face.

The crying stopped as quickly as it had started, replaced by a strange blue light that flickered on and off deeper within the trees. It resembled the beam of a flashlight, only blue in color. She stood stock still, staring and feeling her eyes enlarge as a female figure emerged from the trees and stopped at the edge of the woods. The woman reached out her arms, as if beckoning. Dawn's heart froze in her chest.

Wearing a blue dress with a lace collar, the figure appeared to have silver hair shaped in a bobbed cut. Unable to see her face, which appeared to be covered with a veil, the woman reminded Dawn of the woman in the portrait hanging above the fireplace mantel— Noel's mother. Not believing in ghosts, a shiver, nevertheless, ran down Dawn's spine at the eerie sight.

When a sudden crack of thunder shook the earth, she jumped and her eyes squeezed shut. When they opened again, the ghostly woman was gone, as well as the light. The woods were very dark now.

Light snow began to fall, fat snowflakes swirling through the air and landing in her hair. At the same time, the baby's cry wound up again. Was it really a baby, or an echo Dawn was hearing from a neighbor's house down the road? The sound was not the howl she'd heard before. She cocked her head, listening and trying to determine if the cry was that of a human or animal.

The temperature had dropped considerably since

she returned home earlier in the day. Dawn shivered and hugged herself.

The steady wail combined with the weather convinced her that time was of the essence. If there *was* a child in the woods, for whatever reason, he or she was in distress and needed help immediately. Without a thought to her own warmth and comfort, she ran down the porch steps and sprinted toward the woods.

She couldn't imagine why a baby would be in the woods, unless a homeless person was living out there with her child or someone had abandoned an infant. Unfortunately, either of those scenarios was not all that unusual in today's society.

Dawn followed the cries as she entered the woods and wove her way over downed limbs and through prickly brush. Brittle leaves crunched under her feet and branches poked her in the arms as she rushed forward. The skeleton-like trees closed in on her the deeper she traveled. When the crying suddenly stopped, she stopped, too. Aside from the wind that whistled past her ears, the only noise was the beats of her heart thumping inside her chest.

"Hello?" she tentatively called. "Anyone out here?"

Heavy snow fell harder, dampening her hair and face. Goosebumps skated over her exposed skin. She probably should have put on a coat, but it was more than the cold that had her second-guessing her decision. The hairs on the back of her neck stiffened, and she realized too late that she may have put herself in danger.

The howl of the wolf split the air again. Then

something or someone barged through the trees behind her at full speed. Before she could turn or run in another direction, a hard object came down on her head.

****

The pounding pain was akin to nails being driven into Dawn's skull. Her eyes slowly opened to reveal an ocean of white. A lovely pale face with eyes the color of the sea stared down at her. Golden waves fanned about her head. Her gown was as white as cotton.

"Am I dead?" Dawn asked. "Are you an angel?"

The young woman's pink-tinted lips tilted in a smile. "No, Mrs. Matheson, I'm not an angel. My name is April and I'm a nurse. I've been taking care of you. You're in the Thunder Point Medical Clinic." A soft hand patted Dawn's arm.

Oh. She'd thought she was in heaven. "How long have I been here?" she asked, feeling groggy.

"Three days. We were all so worried, especially your husband. He'll be so happy to know you're awake. He's been at your side the whole time except for quick bathroom and snack breaks. I'll get him and the doctor."

"No." Dawn reached for the nurse's hand, but she slipped away. She may have been discombobulated, but instinct warned that Noel was the last person she wanted to see.

A moment later, he entered the room and rushed to her bedside, followed by a man about his age and build. That man wore a white jacket and a stethoscope

113

hung around his neck, so she assumed he was the doctor.

"Dawn, honey," Noel said, folding her hand into his. "How do you feel?"

She slipped her palm out of his with all the subtlety she could muster. "Like a jackhammer has been breaking up concrete on my head. What happened to me? The nurse said I've been here for three days."

"That's right. You've been in an induced coma. As to what happened to you, I'm afraid it's a bit disturbing."

She gulped. "Tell me, please."

"I was taking a walk through the woods three nights ago when I found you unconscious. What were you doing out there? Do you remember?"

"Let's give her a moment to acclimate, Mr. Matheson," the doctor said. "You can ask questions later." He spent the next few minutes checking her vitals and scribbling into a chart. In that time, Dawn tried to recall what she'd been doing several days earlier that could have possibly landed her in the medical clinic.

By the time the doctor had finished his examination and briefly explained her medical prognosis, she'd remembered hearing the wolf's howl, a baby's cry, and going into the woods next to Noel's parents' house. She also remembered everything Noel had accused her of before that took place. He was a liar. Everything that had transpired between them trickled back in living color.

Once the doctor stepped aside, Noel began his interrogation again.

Instead of answering him, Dawn gazed at the doctor and said, "When can I go home?"

"Although it's more than likely you were hit in the head with a blunt instrument, fortunately, there was no permanent damage to your brain, Mrs. Matheson. We kept you in a coma while the swelling went down. You have a concussion, but rest and time will heal that. I'd like to keep you at the clinic at least another day or two for observation."

"Do you really think that's necessary?" Noel asked.

Dawn glanced at him and noticed him fidgeting, like a caged animal.

The doctor's eyebrows knitted together. "Yes, I do."

Noel forced a smile in her direction. "You heard the doctor, honey. Better safe than sorry. I'll be right here with you until it's time to go home."

Her pulse began to speed up. She wished he would stop calling her honey, and the last thing she wanted was to go home with him when the time came. It was obvious that he wanted to get her back to the house where he could continue to harass her.

"I want to speak to Valerie Bauman," she told the doctor, ignoring Noel. "Will you please call her for me?"

Noel and the doctor exchanged glances.

"Will someone please call her?" she repeated. "Nurse! Where are you?" She glanced around the room, but the sweet nurse had apparently left without her realizing.

"Dawn, why do you want to talk to her?" That was Noel.

Exasperated, her voice lifted, and her stern gaze snapped to him. "Just call her, or bring me my cell phone. Won't you do one simple thing for me, Noel? Why do you insist on making my life so difficult?"

He glanced at the doctor, and his lips tightened in an embarrassed smile. A curt chuckle escaped his lips. "Val is no longer on the island, Dawn. There may not be any way to reach her."

"What do you mean?"

"She left the island the day after you were injured."

"Why?" Her stomach began to roil.

He shrugged. "How would I know? Maybe she got a job in Big Bay, or she left Wisconsin altogether. All I know is she's not on Wolf Island."

"How do you know she left?"

"I heard. Remember, this is a small town. Word gets around fast." He smiled at the doctor.

"I don't believe it," Dawn said. "There was no mention of a new job when we had lunch together. Valerie would have told me she was leaving, or at least contacted me." She glanced around the room. "Where's my purse? I have her number in my purse. I'll call her myself."

"Don't exert yourself, Dawn." When Noel patted her shoulder, she jerked away.

"That's right, Mrs. Matheson," the doctor spoke up. "You must stay calm and keep your blood pressure level and heart rate even."

"We can try to find Val later, after you're feeling better," Noel said.

Frowning, she didn't believe him. She didn't believe a word out of his mouth. "Then I want to speak to Evie."

Once again, Noel and the doctor looked at each other. "I'm afraid there's more bad news," Noel said.

Her shoulders slumped, as if the weight of the world were on them. A premonition of Evie's throat ripped out by the wolf in the woods flashed through her mind. "What happened to her?"

"She had an accident," answered the doctor. "Kicked by one of her horses early this morning. Her knee cap was shattered, so she was air-lifted to Big Bay to the hospital for surgery. I have no doubt she'll come through just fine, but it'll be a long recovery of rehabilitation."

Tears leaked from Dawn's eyes. "Poor Evie." Her head swam. Both Valerie and Evie were unreachable. Who were her allies now? She knew no one else in Thunder Point. There was no one to turn to for advice. No one who would listen and might believe that her husband was gas lighting her—trying to drive her mad. Knotting her hands together, Dawn felt that old familiar hopeless feeling start to sink in. She pulled in a deep breath, determined to fight it. If it was the last thing she did, she'd learn the truth about Noel, Wolf Island, and its secrets, even if it meant her life would change forever.

A voice, smooth and low, drew her attention. She looked up when she heard someone enter the room. Police Chief Cooper, dressed in his usual attire of jeans, a bomber jacket, and a baseball cap sauntered toward her bed and touched the rim of his cap in greeting. His kind face was like a light shining through the dark.

He nodded to both Noel and the doctor, before his gaze latched onto her. "Mrs. Matheson, I received word that you'd woken from the coma. I've been waiting for that good news. I'm here to check on you and ask a few questions."

CHAPTER NINE

Relief flooded Dawn's veins. Chief Cooper—Austin—would help—or at least listen.

"Can I speak to you alone, please?" she asked.

Noel frowned. "Whatever you need to say to him can be said in front of myself and the doctor, Dawn."

"I don't want to talk in front of them," she said, her gaze glued to Austin's, her eyes pleading.

Noel sighed. "You see what I mean about the paranoia, Doctor?"

"I'm not paranoid." Dawn narrowed her eyes and pursed her lips, directing a cold gaze at Noel. "Even if I was, I'd have good reason."

His steel-gray stare warned her to stop.

Austin glanced between her and Noel. " I *would* like to speak to your wife alone, Noel." Noel's chest puffed out and he started to argue, but Austin cut him off. "It's police protocol to speak to the victim of a crime without outside influences or distraction. I'm sure you understand. She has the right to a private interview." He removed a small notebook from his jacket pocket and nodded toward the door, coolly dismissing Noel. "I'll let you and the doctor know when we're finished."

With a grumble, Noel stepped out of the room followed by the doctor.

"Thank you," Dawn said, as soon as the door closed behind them. She stared at the door, wondering if she should whisper, in case someone listened at the door.

Austin must have realized her trepidation. "They're gone," he assured. "I want you to feel free to tell me anything. Let's start by what you remember of that evening you were found in the woods."

In a low voice, her words sprang forth like water bubbling from a fountain. "This is going to sound strange, but my husband is trying to gaslight me. I'm not suggesting he had something to do with the accident—if it was an accident—but I no longer trust him and don't want to be alone with him."

"Gaslight you? What exactly do you mean?" Austin pulled a visitor's chair next to the bed and sat. He unzipped the bomber jacket and then removed his baseball cap and hung it over his knee.

"He's psychologically manipulating me into questioning my own sanity." Dawn went on to quickly explain all the strange incidents that had taken place since they arrived on Wolf Island. Then she told him about her talk with Valerie, and the shocking news that Noel had not only lied to her but also his family. "They never even knew I existed."

For several long beats, Austin stared at her. The expression on his face was one of puzzlement, as if trying to make sense of it. Finally, he spoke. "Any idea why Noel would be doing this to you?"

"None. It was his decision to us move here; he said it would do me good. You see, I've been unsuccessful in carrying a child to term, and Noel thought the change in scenery and lifestyle would relax me." Although she hadn't even been willing to share that information with a counselor, for some odd reason Dawn felt comfortable telling Austin. His face, already holding empathy, softened even more.

"In fact," she continued, "he sold our condo in Chicago without consulting me, which should have been my first sign that something wasn't right. He hasn't been happy for some time. Career wise, he doesn't feel successful, and he wanted a family so badly. At least, I thought he did..." Tears suddenly sprang into her eyes, dampening the fringes of her eyelashes. "I don't know my husband anymore, Austin. Maybe I never knew him at all."

"Do you think he had something to do with the attack on you in the woods? Be honest."

"I would like to think not, but I really don't know. He's changed. He's trying to make me think I'm crazy for some reason, but he's not a violent man. At least, he never has been. I hope that much about him hasn't changed."

"What do you remember before waking up here in the clinic?"

She relayed everything she could recall and then asked, "Do you know anything about Valerie Bauman leaving the island?"

"Can't say that I do."

"What about Evie Rhinehart? Was she taken to a hospital in Big Bay?"

"Yes, her accident came over our radio dispatch. I hear she has to have surgery but that a full recovery is expected."

Dawn breathed a sigh of relief at knowing she'd been told the truth about Evie. However, Valerie's sudden disappearance nagged at her. "I have a bad feeling that Valerie Bauman may be hurt, or worse. She was a patient of Evie's and was living at her facility. I know I shouldn't tell you that because of patient confidentiality, but I'm worried."

"When there's suspicion that a crime may have taken place, nothing is off limits," he said. "You can tell a police officer anything without fear of retribution."

"What a relief. In that case, can you interview the other ladies out there and see what you can find out about Valerie? Ask them if they know whether she left on her own accord. I just don't think she did."

"You bet I will." He jotted a few more notes.

"How did you know I was here?" she asked, suddenly curious.

"The clinic called my office when you were brought in. It's protocol whenever there are suspicious circumstances surrounding an accident."

"I see. And my accident was suspicious."

"Yes. Someone purposefully assaulted you. You were knocked unconscious by a hard object and left alone. If Noel hadn't come along when he did…well, who knows what condition you'd be in now."

She uttered a small gasp. Although the doctor had told her she'd suffered a concussion, understanding that she'd been the target of a vicious attack hadn't struck until now. Her throat went dry and she couldn't catch her breath.

Austin jumped up from the chair and quickly poured a glass of water from the pitcher setting on the moveable tray next to her bed. "Here, drink this," he said, placing the glass to her lips.

She drank and then laid her head back against the pillow. Neither of them spoke for a few moments.

"Are you okay?" he asked.

She nodded. "Yes. It all just became so real. I felt like I was going to hyperventilate. Thank you for the water."

"You're welcome."

"Do you have more to tell?"

"A bit. I immediately interviewed Noel and went to the area in the woods where he claimed to have discovered you. Unfortunately, I found no evidence of the weapon used in your attack. It could have been a tree limb, but they're all over the ground out there and there's no way to lift prints from natural wood. Even though it snowed that day, we found nothing resembling footprints. I hate to say it, but I'm afraid we're at a dead end unless you can remember something more."

She shook her head. "Sorry I can't." After a moment, "Oh, wait! There *is* something, but I hesitate to tell you. You might think I *am* crazy."

"I'd never think that. Not in a million years." He stared at her until physiology forced him to blink.

The intensity with which he met her gaze caused the beats of her heart to drum inside her chest. For some reason, she trusted him completely. Dawn told him about the ghostly woman.

He didn't laugh or even smile. Austin respectfully listened and included the description in his notebook. "Is that all?"

"Yes, I think so."

"When do you leave the clinic?" he asked, snapping the notebook shut.

"The doctor wants me to stay one or two more nights for observation."

Austin nodded. "When I leave here I'll immediately start investigating Val Bauman's whereabouts and come back tomorrow to let you know what I've learned."

"Thank you so much." She reached for his hand and squeezed it to show her appreciation. His touch warmed her chilled skin, and he squeezed back, grasping her hand as if he never wanted to let go. The top of his open shirt below his unzipped jacket gave her a view of the pulse beating in his neck. When he caught her staring, the wisp of a smile crinkled his lips, and the low, rich sound of his voice sent a flame sizzling through her.

She extracted her hand from his slowly and smiled.

Austin cleared his throat. "Before I go, I want to tell you what I discovered about that dead animal you found on your front porch steps."

She scooted to a more comfortable sitting position. "Yes? What about it?" So much had happened since then, she'd nearly forgotten that Austin had taken care of that awful mess.

"I had tests run on it before disposing of the carcass. As I suspected, it was a dog, not a wolf. The strange thing is, Pentobarbital was found in its stomach. Do you know what that is?"

"No. I've never owned a dog."

"It's euthanasia medication that most vets use. The dog was put down before its throat was ripped out."

123

Her eyebrows furrowed, not understanding. "Are you saying a vet gave the dog the medication and then another animal attacked it? Could that even be possible?"

"No, it's not possible. A dog who has been administered Pentobarbital passes away within moments. It's not the kind of medicine a vet sends home with a client to administer. There's no way another animal could have possibly attacked it."

"Then, how it came to land on our steps doesn't make sense."

"No, it doesn't. But it's possible a vet didn't administer the drug at all. Someone else might have."

The dire implication of his words had her sitting up even straighter in the bed.

Austin explained. "According to the veterinarian I consulted with, the dog's neck was torn out *after* it was already dead. Just like a doctor who performs human autopsies, vets have a way of knowing these things. The weirdest part is, another animal was not the perpetrator. Because of the shape and depth of the injury, the vet could tell that the damage was not caused by a canine's teeth. The wounds were not like those caused by another animal at all. His guess is that some sort of contraption, like a trap with claws, was used to tear out the throat."

Dawn wrinkled her nose at the image. "You've got me really confused now."

"I was, too, until another expert I talked to explained a possible scenario to me. I called a psychiatrist friend of mine who practices in Big Bay to get his take on what we might have. According to him, it could be a case of lycanthropy."

"What's that?"

"A rare psychiatric disorder. There are apparently people who suffer the delusion of being able to transform into a non-human animal. My friend has read a study on lycanthropy from a well-known psychiatric hospital in Massachusetts that reported on a series of cases. A person with this syndrome believes he or she is in the process of transforming into an animal or has already transformed into an animal. The affected person even behaves in a manner that resembles animal behavior. For example, by growling, crawling on all fours, and howling."

Dawn's mouth dropped open. "Like a wolf?"

"It's possible that the howls you've heard in the woods could actually be a person who thinks he's a wolf," Austin confirmed.

A violent shudder wracked her body. "That's one of the strangest and most frightening things I've ever heard."

"I agree." He skimmed a hand through his short-cropped hair. "One of the cases my friend read about was of a man in 1908 who used a device very similar to a trap with claws to murder several young women in the Whitechapel district of London. Those murders took place twenty years after the Jack the Ripper cases, which also occurred in Whitechapel. There were other similarities that had the police wondering if Jack the Ripper had returned, but ultimately, the murderer was caught, confessed, and it was determined that he suffered from lycanthropy."

A thought occurred to her. "If there's someone like that here in Thunder Point, that person may have been the one who attacked me in the woods." She gulped. "Are you saying I could have been murdered?"

Austin's hand covered hers and he gazed deep into her eyes once again. "That's not what I'm suggesting at all, Dawn. But whoever did this to you came pretty close to killing you." He shook his head. "Hell, I don't know if the mangled dog on your porch steps and your assault are even connected. I sense you're a strong woman. You'd have to be very strong to have gotten past what you went through in Chicago. And now, the things that have happened here..." His voice trailed off. "I thought you'd want to know what I learned. That's all." His sympathetic gaze delved deeper. "I'm sorry if I've upset you. That's the last thing I intended."

She breathed in and out several times to gain composure. Austin believed she was a strong woman. The man had no idea what hearing that meant to her. She *was* strong and getting more so every day. Whatever was happening on Wolf Island, and whatever game Noel was playing for whatever sick reason, she wouldn't let any of it make her forget what she was made of.

"You're right, Austin. I do want to know everything you find out. You're the only one I can turn to, the only person I completely trust right now. Thank you for helping me."

He smiled. "Just doing my job, ma'am."

As the Chief of Police, that was true, of course, but something in his gaze suggested more. A deeper connection was forging between them. He was a new friend, someone she absolutely could count on.

His voice was soft and caring when he said, "Get some rest and I'll see you tomorrow." He touched her hand.

"All right."

He snugged the baseball cap over his head and said, "I don't mind you knowing, I was pretty worried when I heard you'd been hurt."

"You were?"

"Well, sure. If word got out that someone was going around bopping pretty ladies on the head, it could affect tourism." A mischievous grin quirked his lips, and she smiled in return.

"Seriously, though. I came by immediately the day you were brought in, but the staff said I couldn't see you until you woke up. I'm relieved to see with my own eyes that you're all right. Take my word, Dawn, I'll work day and night until I find the culprit that hurt you. I promise that person will be locked up and justice will be served." He tipped his cap and sauntered out the door with a gait as confident as John Wayne's.

When Noel returned to her bedside a few moments later, Dawn said she was tired and wanted to nap. She had no desire to talk to him or pretend she was glad he was there.

She expected he'd give her the third degree and press her on what she'd told Austin. But when she rolled over and gave him her back, he got the message and said goodbye.

"Get some rest and I'll see you tomorrow."

Hearing the exact same words that Austin had just spoken sent a jolt through her. However, the intonation in Noel's parting goodbye was completely different. There was something important missing from Noel's farewell that had rang clear and true from Austin—a sincere concern for her wellbeing.

127

CHAPTER TEN

The next afternoon, Austin dropped in to see Dawn, as promised. She knew it was wrong, because she was married, but the moment she laid eyes on him, giddiness spread through her like the scent of honeysuckle on a fine spring day.

The friendly blonde nurse had just taken Dawn's blood pressure when he walked in. "Good morning, Chief," she greeted.

"Mornin', Nurse Simpsen."

April finished writing in Dawn's chart and then tucked a fresh blanket around her waist and winked. "Ring your buzzer if you need anything, Mrs. Matheson."

"I will. Thank you, April."

Once the nurse left the room, Austin pulled up a chair and sat. "Your color has returned. Your face was pale yesterday, but your cheeks are pink today. I take that as a good sign. How are you feeling today?"

"Much better, despite having nightmares last night."

"Tell me about them."

"I dreamt a wolf chased me through the woods and caught me. He pounced on my chest and began clawing at my throat. While I was screaming, the face of the wolf morphed into Noel's face. His teeth were bloody fangs. I woke up just as his fangs were about to plunge into my neck. I know he was about to kill me."

Austin touched her arm, sending a zing of electricity racing up it. "It was just a bad dream. I won't let anyone hurt you again."

She smiled, but felt self-conscious at the tender way he spoke. Although Noel had betrayed her in many ways, he was still her husband. Austin was a friend, but more than that, he was the man paid to protect the citizens of Thunder Point—and she was one of them. That was all his comment had meant. Nothing more. Changing the subject, she said, "Did you find Valerie?"

He shook his head. "No luck so far. I interviewed the ladies out at Evie's place and none of them knew of any plans Val had to leave. When I searched her room, everything appeared to be in place. Clothes were hanging in the closet and her suitcases were there. Even her purse was on her bed. But we found no cell phone."

Unease snuck along Dawn's chest wall. "Leaving her purse proves she wasn't expecting to go far or she didn't go of her own free will. No woman leaves her purse behind."

"Just what I thought. I would have called Val's phone to see if she answered, but none of the ladies at the barn had her number. I contacted the hospital in Big Bay to reach Evie, figuring she has the number, but she was in surgery, so I left a message with the nurse's station there."

"I've got Val's number!" Dawn said. "It's on a

slip of paper she gave to me the day we had lunch together. The paper's in my purse. But my purse must still be at the house. Noel never brought it to me."

"I'll check with him and ask to see your purse. He is at home now?"

"As far as I know. He was here earlier this morning, but left around ten o'clock. I wasn't in the mood to talk."

Austin nodded, seeming to understand. "In the meantime, something else just came up that I'm sure you'll be interested in," he said.

"What's that?"

"Keith Matheson is back in town. I saw him getting off the ferry as I was driving over here."

"Noel's brother? I wonder why he's returned to the island. Do you think he might know where Valerie is? Or maybe he has something to do with her disappearance? They apparently didn't part on good terms."

"I'll track him down and ask a few questions. Do you think he's heard you and Noel moved back and he's come home to make amends? The two of them also didn't part well the last time they were together."

Dawn shrugged. "I have no idea. I've never met Keith before, but from what Noel has said, the brothers haven't gotten along for years. Noel doesn't talk about him except to complain and criticize."

"What does Noel complain about?"

"Well, he has said Keith was always causing trouble while they were growing up. He hung with a bad crowd in high school, smoked marijuana and drank. Said he was gone from the house a lot and didn't help with family chores, that sort of thing.

Apparently, he and their father didn't get along because of it. I guess Noel has never forgiven Keith for his mistakes of the past."

"Really? From what I recall, it was the other way around."

"What do you mean the other way around?"

Austin rubbed his chin thoughtfully. "I probably shouldn't have said anything, but from what you told me yesterday, you've been lied to enough."

Dawn braced for more bad news. "Go ahead, Austin, and tell me what you know."

"It's just that Noel was the brother that stirred up trouble in school, in town, and even at home. As you might expect, there aren't many secrets in Thunder Point, so everyone within a few years of him knew the situation. His dad was a tough man and Noel rebelled. They didn't get along for years, and then Noel was kicked off the football team for drug use. From rumors at the time, that was the straw that broke the camel's back, as they say. Apparently, his father never forgave him for screwing up his chances at a scholarship. Noel was the more athletic of the brothers, and it was expected he'd earn a college football scholarship and maybe even play in the big leagues someday. He was supposed to be the golden boy and make something of himself."

All the air left Dawn's lungs. "I had no idea." Although Noel still owed her an explanation, maybe she'd discovered the reason for the strained relationship between him and his family. "He did make something of himself," she said, softly. "He may not have been a pro football player and he's not financially wealthy, but he's been a decent man and he was successful in many ways. His father should have been proud of him, regardless."

Suddenly, she felt her heart softening for the man she'd fallen in love with. "He didn't need to lie to me—about any of it. If he'd told me the truth, I would have understood. That's all water under the bridge anyway. It was so long ago. I'm not a psychologist, but I might have been able to do something to help bring the family together again and help them heal. Noel's parents may have enjoyed having another daughter-in-law. My own parents are both gone. I would have liked having a family again."

"I know the Mathesons would have welcomed you with open arms," Austin replied. "They would have loved you." When her eyes widened with surprise at his heartfelt comment, he quickly continued. "What I mean is, you're a very likeable person. I don't know why Noel lied. That's something he'll have to explain. But don't be too quick to forget all that he's put you through in the last few days. By your own admission, he's gas lighting you, and we need to determine why and fast. That's not loving husband behavior."

Dawn felt embarrassed, knowing he was right.

"I'm not convinced it's safe for you to stay in the same house," Austin said. "Just yesterday you told me you're afraid to be alone with him."

"Yes, I did, but maybe I was too quick to judge. I really don't think he had anything to do with what happened to me in the woods."

"Maybe you don't *want* to believe it." Austin cocked a brow. "The nightmare you had could be your subconscious mind talking. You would do good to listen."

"You're right. I don't want to believe my husband is trying to drive me mad on purpose. Or that he could hurt me. Like you told me yesterday, it was just a bad dream."

"But the gas lighting. That's nothing to forget and forgive so easily. Only someone cruel and demented would do that to the person they supposedly love."

Dawn heard the passion in Austin's voice and was grateful for his concern. He was only doing his job, after all.

"I hear everything you're saying, Austin, and I take it to heart. I really do. I was so hurt and angry yesterday that I wanted nothing more to do with Noel. But I realize I do have to talk with him and clear the air. If he's honest about why he lied to me and his family, I'll give him a chance to make things right. I don't know that our relationship will ever be the same, but we've been married three years. I had the opportunity to leave him before we moved here, but he's my husband. I can't just walk away without knowing why he's done what he's done."

"Have you considered that he's mentally disturbed?" Austin asked.

She nodded. "I did a lot of thinking yesterday. There's not much else to do when you're stuck in a hospital bed. If he's got psychological problems, I'll get him the help he needs."

Austin heaved a deep sigh. "That's honorable, but just remember, the ones closest to us are usually the ones who cut the deepest. I've seen it time and again in my profession."

"I'll keep that in mind." She offered her hand to shake. "Thank you for all your help. Please let me know if you're able to track down Keith. I'd like to meet him and see if there's any chance that he and Noel can reconcile."

"I wouldn't hold my breath," Austin said. "When you get out of here, promise me you'll keep an eye out at all times."

She drew an invisible X over her heart with a finger. "I promise."

"And call me if you need anything at all. Day or night, I'll come running. And by all means do not go back into the woods. The person who attacked you is probably still on the island and could still be lurking around Noel's property."

They were shaking hands just as Noel walked through the door. His big smile dissolved upon seeing the police chief.

"Austin, what are you doing here?"

"Updating Mrs. Matheson on our investigation into her assault."

"Have you got someone in custody yet?"

"No, but we're working on it." He slid a sideways glance at Dawn. Apparently, he wasn't going to update Noel on the lycanthropy theory he'd mentioned yesterday or bring up his investigation into Valerie's whereabouts.

Dawn noticed Noel held a tote bag in his arms. "Did you bring me clothes?" she asked.

"Yeah. You'll need them when you're released."

"Did you happen to bring my purse, too?"

He dug it out of the bag and carried it to her, giving Austin the once over as he passed.

Dawn unzipped the purse and searched for the slip of paper Valerie had given her.

"What are you looking for?" Noel asked.

"Valerie gave me her cell phone number the other day. It was on a slip of paper, but I can't find it now." She turned the purse upside down and dumped its contents next to her on the bed. "Chief Cooper is trying to get a hold of her and no one has her number. I had it. What could have happened to it?"

"Are you sure Val gave it to you?" Noel asked. His eyebrow arched.

Dawn froze. He was doing it again—trying to make her think she was losing her mind. "She gave it to me," she said, voice hard as glass. "Maybe you removed the paper from my purse before you brought it here."

Noel laughed and shook his head. "What on earth are you talking about, Dawn?"

Austin jumped in. "Don't worry about it Dawn, er, Mrs. Matheson. I'll track down Val's number. You get some rest and I'll check in with you again tomorrow to give you another update."

Noel's eyes narrowed. "Thanks for stopping by, Chief."

Austin ignored his icy glare and held out his hand to shake. "No problem, Noel. Don't let your wife out of your sight. From all accounts, her attack was not random. Chances are likely she was the target."

Noel moved to the other side of the hospital bed and began returning the items on the bed to Dawn's purse. "I'm perfectly capable of taking care of my wife, Chief Cooper. But I do appreciate the advice."

Dawn turned her head and gave Austin a look that spoke volumes. She mouthed, "I'm sorry."

"By the way, Noel. In case you didn't know, your

brother's in town. Maybe he's come to make amends with you or his ex. That is, if Val's still in Thunder Point."

Dawn felt Noel's body go rigid beside her. His hand clutched her arm and he squeezed tight. "I have nothing to say to my brother, Chief. As for Valerie Bauman, good luck finding her."

The tone of his voice caused the hair on Dawn's scalp to prickle. Her gaze caught with Austin's again. He looked as if he wanted to say something more, but he bit back a retort, tipped his cap, and left.

"Good news," Noel said, drawing her attention away from the door. "The doctor says you can go home."

"When?"

"Today. Now."

She tilted her head. "I thought he wanted me to stay at least another day."

He hurriedly began to withdraw clothes from the bag. "He says you're good to go and he's releasing you today."

"But yesterday—"

"Yesterday he said a day or two. It's been a day and we're going home. Go ahead and put on your clothes." He thrust a pair of jeans and sweater at her.

"Why are you in such a hurry?" she asked.

"I'm not. I thought you'd want to get out of here as quickly as possible and get back to your own home and bed. That's all."

Just then, April walked in carrying a folder. "Looks like you're being released, Mrs. Matheson." She didn't wear her usual friendly smile, and her expression went sour at seeing Noel.

"Yes, my husband just told me." An icy thread wound up Dawn's spine. Noel was too anxious to get her out of there. April, clearly, was not happy, and the doctor was nowhere in sight.

"I have your discharge papers right here," April said. She handed Dawn a couple of sheets and went over the instructions. "The doctor has written a prescription that's stronger than Tylenol for your pain. You'll probably have a headache off and on for the next few days, but if you develop any other symptoms, such as vertigo or nausea, call the clinic immediately."

"I will."

The nurse left the room briefly and returned with a wheelchair.

"I don't need that, do I?" Dawn asked.

"Sorry, but it's the rules, Mrs. Matheson. I'll wheel you out after you've dressed."

"I can wheel her out," Noel said.

April shot him an annoyed glance.

The tension in the air was as thick as pea soup. Dawn suspected Noel had strong-armed the doctor into releasing her early and April knew. Why else would the nurse act so perturbed? "Noel, why don't you bring the car around?" she suggested. "As soon as I'm dressed, April can wheel me out."

Thankfully, he acquiesced.

At the curb, Dawn gave April a hug. "Thank you for taking good care of me."

"It was a pleasure, Mrs. Matheson." She cut a quick glance at the Jeep and said, "Let us know if you need anything, and good luck."

Dawn stifled a bitter laugh. She might need more than luck to get through the night with Noel. It was her plan to have a heart-to-heart with him.

****

Staring out the car window, Dawn felt a spasm in her stomach. Noel's response to Austin had sounded ominous. What had he meant, good luck finding Valerie? Did he know where she was? Had he threatened her and scared her off the island? Or was the comment meant to be sincere even if it came across as rude? And why had he convinced the doctor to release her a day early? There could be no good reason, except that he was up to his old tricks again.

Maybe it was a bad idea to go home with him, after all. But she had nowhere else to go. The only two people she might have been able to spend the night with were gone.

As Noel drove through town, two women arguing in front of the market caught Dawn's attention. She opened her mouth to make a comment and closed it just as fast when she realized the women were Noel's school friends, Madeline and Leslie. Clearly, the shorter, blonde Leslie was highly agitated. Her hands motioned wildly, and she appeared to be doing all the talking. Suddenly, the statuesque Madeline poked Leslie in the chest with her finger several times. Her mouth twisted into a snarl and said something that caused Leslie to step back. When Dawn cut a quick glance at Noel, it seemed he hadn't noticed them. His gaze was focused straight ahead. When she looked out the window again, Leslie was crying and walking in the opposite direction.

I wonder what that was about.

Noel parked in front of the drug store. "I'll run in and get your prescription filled," he said. "Shouldn't take long."

"All right, thanks."

He leaned over and gave her a kiss on the cheek. "It'll be good to have you home again. The house has been quiet without you."

She nodded, hearing the kind words and noting the smile on his face but not fully believing the sentiment.

Austin's words replayed through her mind.

Don't be too quick to forget all that he's put you through. He's gas lighting you and we need to find out why.

She laid her head back against the seat and closed her eyes, wondering what options she had besides going home. None, unless she chose to stay in a motel. That would only aggravate Noel more, and he probably wouldn't let her have the Jeep. No way would he agree to drop her off and leave her. Unfortunately, she had to go home with him, but there would be no more games. They'd have a serious talk. The first thing she'd force from him would be the truth about his relationship with his family.

If he was honest with her and satisfactorily explained the lies, that was one thing. But there weren't any excuses satisfactory enough to forgive his recent behavior. He'd emotionally abused her and to what end? Why had he done it?

It was possible she could eventually forgive him—if he got help. But she would not forget his treatment of her, as Austin had reminded. And she didn't see how they could continue a relationship let alone their marriage. No longer was she naïve or blinded by a love that may have never been real. It was obvious Noel had a mental problem. Or a very flawed moral system. Either way, Dawn could not live with him any longer. The marriage was over.

Inhaling a deep breath, it felt like the weight of the world had been lifted from her shoulders.

But she couldn't just walk out tonight. It would take a bit of planning to figure out where to go and how to get there—and how to do it without antagonizing him. No longer could she trust his reactions or loyalty.

Laughter outside the vehicle grabbed her attention. When she opened her eyes, her gaze locked on a couple kissing right on the sidewalk in front of her. And it wasn't just a simple goodbye kiss either. It was the type of kiss a man deeply in love—or lust—gives a woman. Spellbound by their unbridled passion, Dawn stared open-mouthed, though she did have the decency to slide down further in her seat so as not to come across as a peeping Tom if anyone saw her watching.

When they parted, she was surprised to recognized the man. It was Madeline Reed's boyfriend. Carl was his name. Another high school acquaintance of Noel's. Only this wasn't Madeline he had just kissed. He pinched the curly redhead's bottom through her coat, and she giggled before turning and sashaying the other direction with a huge smile on her face.

Carl stared after her until she rounded the corner. Then he stepped through the door of the building in front of him. The sign above the door read: Thunder Point Veterinary Clinic.

Funny, he didn't have an animal with him.

The drug store door opened and Noel held up a paper sack as he approached the Jeep. "Got it," he said, as he climbed in and slammed the door. "And I brought you a surprise."

Great. Hadn't there been enough surprises for one day? He dug into the bag and extracted a packet of Turtle candies, her favorite. "A sweet for my sweet."

The act was thoughtful, though odd considering the strain between them. Still, she would be polite so as not to raise any suspicion. "Thank you, Noel."

"You're welcome. Is there anything else you need before we head home?"

She shook her head. What she could really use was one night without drama. But that would likely not be the case.

CHAPTER ELEVEN

As Noel pulled into their drive, Dawn mentioned that she saw Carl kiss a woman other than Madeline. "They said they were dating when we met them at the café. Remember?"

He shrugged. "They're probably not exclusive."

"Mmm. They were pretty touchy feely that evening, as I recall. Madeline seems like the kind of woman who wouldn't like her guy making out with another woman, especially in public. What do you think?"

"How would I know what Maddie would put up with?"

"I didn't say—oh, never mind." Tired of his surly attitude, she didn't wait for him to come around and open her door. Striding across the barren lawn and up the porch steps, her head felt woozy by the time she reached the front door. An invisible thread pulled at her, but she refused to look across the porch toward the woods. She shivered, realizing once again how lucky she was to have come out of there with only a concussion.

"It's freezing," Noel said, slipping his key in the lock. "The temperature is dropping fast." When she stepped inside, he said, "I'll get some wood from the shed. Feels like the perfect evening for a crackling fire. Would you like that?"

"Sure. That would be nice." It *was* very cold out, so for once they agreed on something. The warmth and ambiance of a fire might make the conversation she planned on having easier to swallow.

He set the tote bag on the foyer floor. "Get settled and I'll be in shortly. I'll bring in the wood and then make you a hot cup of tea."

As Dawn hung her coat up on the hall tree, she sighed. Noel's personality shifts had worn thin. At least she wouldn't have long to put up with the stress. Once they had their discussion, she'd decide on the best time to tell him she wanted a divorce. With all this swimming around in her head, she stepped into the kitchen and filled a kettle with hot water to boil. She could make her own tea.

After she freshened up and changed into sweat pants to be more comfortable, she went downstairs to find him sitting in front of the fireplace adding a log to the roaring fire. There was also a steaming cup of tea sitting on the end table. Obviously, he had gone ahead and made her tea instead of waiting for her to do it. He craned his head over his shoulder and smiled. "You look comfy."

"Well, I realize it's only three o'clock in the afternoon, but I'm exhausted." She sat on the sofa, curled her legs underneath her, and sniffed the teacup. "This smells delicious. Chamomile?"

"Yes. It's your favorite."

"So it is." She took a sip and savored the sweet apple flavor on her tongue. Noticing a mug of coffee on the other end table, she invited him to sit on the sofa. "Sit and enjoy the fire."

"Don't mind if I do." He rose and settled into the sofa cushions and sipped at the coffee.

For several moments, Dawn stared into the fire thinking of all the things she wanted to say and how to begin. Yes, Noel had been mostly on good behavior today, but that didn't excuse him from everything else he'd put her through. Austin's words continued to play through her mind like a broken record. There were plenty of questions that needed to be answered. She wrapped her hands around the teacup and softly said, "Do you think your brother has returned to the island to make amends with you?"

Noel's gaze briefly went dark, but he recovered quickly. His tone was agreeable but seemed forced when he answere., "I don't know, Dawn. The last time we saw each other, heated words were exchanged."

"And you nearly got into a fist fight, from what I heard."

"Who told you that?" When she didn't reply— only stared—he said, "Never mind. It could have been anyone. Gossip runs rampant in this town. That's one of the reasons I left in the first place."

She pressed on. "He's your only brother, Noel. Maybe the two of you could at least talk. Whatever went wrong, it couldn't have been so bad that your relationship can't be repaired. You only have each other now. I'm sure your parents would rest easier knowing you'd forgiven each other."

His chest rose and fell in a deep sigh. After several beats, he said, "If it's that important to you, I'll be the bigger man and reach out to Keith, but I can't promise he'll be receptive. I'm not even sure where to find him."

"As you've said many times, Thunder Point is a small town. It shouldn't be hard to track him down."

So badly she wanted to tell him that Austin had confided in her with the truth. She knew that Noel was the problem, not Keith, but placing blame right then would get her nowhere. She had to make him believe she still trusted him, just in case he knew something about Valerie's whereabouts. A more than nagging suspicion that he did continued to sour her stomach.

"Are you hungry?" he asked. "I can make us some sandwiches."

"I could eat, but I don't mind fixing them. You've already been a great help today. And you've held down the fort while I was in the clinic." The words tasted bitter on her tongue, but it was easier to catch flies with honey than with vinegar, as the old saying went. It was better to butter him up before throwing the hammer down. However, when she stood up, the room began to spin and she collapsed back onto the sofa.

"Dawn, what is it?" He scooted to her side and placed his hand on her forehead. "You're hot."

Of course she was hot; they were sitting in front of a blazing fire. "I'll be all right. I'm just a little dizzy."

"The doctor said you'll have headaches for a few more days. Let me get that prescription medicine."

It was true; her head was starting to pound. "All right. Good idea."

He left and returned a minute later with two tablets and a glass of water. "Down the hatch. You'll feel better in no time." He dropped the pills into her palm.

For some reason, it felt like she had no control over her hand. The pills slipped out of her palm onto the floor. When he body began to tingle, her eyes enlarged.

"Noel, I feel very strange. The room is spinning and my head…"

He dropped to his knees and stuck his face in hers, studying her like she was a bug under a microscope.

It wasn't long before she felt so drowsy she couldn't keep her eyes open. Her eyelids grew as heavy as iron.

"My arms feel… like lead." She tried to lift a hand and couldn't.

He patted her knee. "You'll be okay. Don't fight it. It'll be better that way."

Fight what? "Those pills… really… work… fast." Her tongue felt like cotton, and it was hard to speak. In fact, she wasn't sure she had spoken out loud at all. Maybe the words were only in her mind. Suddenly she remembered she hadn't even taken the pills yet.

Her ears felt plugged. The noises around her—the fire cracking and popping, and Noel talking to her—sounded muted, like she was under water.

She felt a pillow slip under her head and Noel's hands moved over her body. He was laying her horizontal on the sofa. But why? His face hovered over hers for a moment, and his lips moved, but she couldn't hear him. She blinked several times. Then his face vanished from in front of her. Closing her eyes, she allowed heaviness to wash over her.

Someone shook her arm. Noel peered into her face again. "How do you feel?" he asked.

She had no idea how long she'd been asleep. But

this time she heard her own small voice reply, "Tired." It was all she could manage.

"Sit up," he ordered.

Arms slipped behind her back and hauled her to a sitting position. Barely able to hold up her own body weight, her head lolled onto her neck. Noel sat next to her and lifted her hand. Something hard and thin was placed between her fingers. "Hold it tighter," he barked. Her eyes flew open at his voice, only to involuntarily drift shut again. No matter how hard she tried, she could not keep them open. All she wanted to do was sleep.

The feel of something hard and flat was pressed to her lap. Was it a board of some kind? The sound of rustling papers briefly roused her again. Noel's hand wrapped around hers and he began guiding her hand across the paper. "Sign this," he said, "and you can go back to sleep."

Mustering all the strength she had, she turned her head and focused on his glistening face. Sweat trickled into his wide eyes, and his lips compressed into a tight line. "Sign this," he demanded again. "I'll help you." Again, she felt his hand bear down and try to guide hers.

Her head dropped and her gaze moved across the paper on her lap. The words on the paper blurred, running together like rain on ink. "What...is...this?"

Before he answered, the sound of a cell phone ring pierced the air. The ring startled her, but there was no physical response. Unable to move even a muscle, her chest tightened, her heart beat faster, and she wanted to scream. But no sound came out of her mouth. She couldn't even open her mouth. Her entire body felt frozen.

"Just sign it, dammit it!" Noel shouted. He pressed her hand down even harder.

When the cell phone continued to blare, Noel muttered, "Shit" and finally released her hand. "Hello," he snapped.

Without his help to hold her up, Dawn slumped over. Although her eyes were closed and her eyelids felt glued shut, she used every bit of power she could muster to concentrate on the noises around her. She had no idea why she felt so strange. Her brain felt in a fog. Her thoughts were jumbled, but she was aware enough to know that something was very wrong. If she guessed correctly, Noel had put something in her tea. Feeling like she was sinking to the bottom of the deep, dark lake, terror strummed her nerves. She wanted to cry out but was unable to utter a sound.

Reaching for calm, she forced herself to concentrate on his phone conversation.

"She's too drugged to sign," he mumbled. Then after a pause, "I tried! I'm doing what I can. I got her out of the clinic today, which is what you wanted."

Using all her might, Dawn squeezed open one eye to see Noel pacing the living room floor with his cell phone to his ear. Nervously raking his hand through his hair, he reminded her of a trapped animal.

"It's going to take more time, Maddie," he hissed.

Dawn's breath caught in her clogged throat. *Maddie*?

"It's not going to happen tonight," he said. "I'll have to figure out something else. Just give me a minute to think!"

He stomped out of the room, giving Dawn time to process what she'd just heard. She was right to have been afraid. Noel, her husband, had been conspiring against her. But to what end? Whatever the reason, he'd given her something to immobilize her! Perhaps he planned to kill her. If he tried, she wouldn't be able to defend herself.

Had he been the one to knock her unconscious in the woods, after all? Or had it been Madeline? Had they intended on her dying that day? Obviously, they were in this together—whatever this was.

Suddenly, his voice grew louder and he returned to the living room. It appeared he didn't care whether Dawn heard or not. Probably, he thought she was too drugged to know what was going on around her. Unable to move and exhausted from concentrating so hard, her eyes drifted shut again. But she kept listening.

"What do you mean you're going to get rid of them? Oh, God, Maddie, this is not what we agreed to. Don't do anything drastic. Do you hear me?" There was another pause. Then, "I said no! Hang tight. I'm coming over right now. Keep your head!"

A moment later, the conversation ended. Noel continued to pace the room for a few seconds. Then Dawn could sense him standing over her, heat and sweat emanating off his body. Physically, there was nothing she could do to protect herself, so she emotionally braced for an impact of some sort. Believing her life was about to be snuffed out by the hands of the man she had once loved, she sent a silent prayer to God, asking Him to let death come quickly.

Instead of feeling hands on her throat, however, Noel snatched the paper off the sofa and Dawn heard his footfalls move out of the room. The front door slammed shut, tires sped out of the driveway, and she was alone—and paralyzed.

CHAPTER TWELVE

Loud pounding on the front door intruded upon her strange dreams. Stirring, Dawn awoke to the kind of confusion a person feels when she's slept very deeply. For several moments, she had no recollection of where she was. There was no panic, only a comfortable confusion. If she remained very still and was patient, everything would sort itself out, she was sure.

She opened her eyes and looked around, trying to identify the room—realized it was the living room—and tried to remember why she was there and not in her bed.

Memory came back slowly, the sound of a crackling fire, the smell of fear and sweat, a figure pacing the floor talking loudly, and then a face hovering over her.

She sat up and crossed her arms over her prone body. The room was freezing and so was she. No wonder. There was no blanket covering her. Turning her head, she saw that the fireplace was cold and black embers filled the grate.

Body stiff and sore, there was a pain in her neck and her head throbbed.

More pounding on wood roused her. Someone was at the front door. "Coming," she called. Finding her legs, she shuffled to the foyer. "Noel?" The word came out croaking at first. She swallowed and tried again. "Noel?"

No answer. The house felt eerily deserted.

"Mrs. Matheson," a voice outside the door hollered. Then more urgently, "Dawn, are you in there?"

Recognizing the voice, she pulled the door open, noticing it wasn't locked, and blinked several times, trying to focus on the police chief's face—Austin's handsome unshaven face, scruffy with a day's growth. Her gaze moved to another man standing next to him.

"Dawn, are you all right?" Austin didn't wait to be invited in; he stepped inside and gently guided her away from the door. The other man followed. Before that man closed the door behind them, she peered outside and realized the ground was white and snow was falling thickly from the sky.

Austin placed his finger under her chin and lifted it to stare into her eyes. "Are you all right?"

"I…think so. But I'm so cold."

He grabbed a sweater from off the coat tree and wrapped her in it. Staring into her eyes, he said, "What happened to you?"

"I... I don't know. I just woke up." Bits and pieces of what seemed like a movie reel rolled through her mind.

"Are you hurt?" With urgency, he pulled up the sleeves of the sweater and checked her arms, then her neck and head for marks and bruises. Feeling like putty under his warm hands, she stared at the cords on his neck, flexing and quivering.

"I don't think so. I'm so tired, though. What time is it?"

"Eight o'clock,"

"At night?" As soon as the words tumbled from her mouth, she knew they were not right. It was light outside, not dark.

"No, Dawn, it's eight in the morning."

Memories began to slowly creep to the surface. Slowly calculating when she and Noel had gotten home yesterday, she remembered sitting in front of the fire, a headache coming on, feeling dizzy, and him bringing her medicine. Before that, she'd drunk tea that he'd prepared.

Reality spurned her into the present. "I've been out for sixteen hours!"

The other man finally spoke up. "Where's Noel?"

"Dawn, this is Keith Matheson, Noel's brother," Austin said.

"Oh." She reached out to shake his hand, which he took. "You're my brother-in-law."

"Yeah, I guess I am. Sorry we had to meet under these circumstances though. I don't mean to be rude, but do you know where my brother is right now?"

She raked her hand through her tangled hair. "I don't think he's in the house. I called before I came to the door and he didn't answer. Is the Jeep outside?"

Austin shook his head. "Can we sit down and talk?"

"Of course." She was almost beginning to feel normal. After leading them to the living room, she offered them coffee, but both declined.

"Do you remember I told you Keith had come back to the island?" Austin began.

152

"Yes." She glanced at Noel's brother and realized there wasn't much of a physical resemblance between them.

"Well, he's here because he's worried about Valerie. He received a distress call on his cell phone from her the same day you were attacked in the woods. Since then, he's been trying to reach her on her cell with no luck. That's why he decided to return to Thunder Point."

"She said 'help me' and she also mentioned my brother's name before the phone went dead," Keith added.

Dawn felt the pace of her heart speed up. "Oh, no." She slapped a hand over her mouth. The memory of what Noel had put her through the night before came back in a rush. Anger flared at remembering the terror she'd felt at being paralyzed and afraid for her life.

Like bullets from a gun, the chain of events flew from her mouth in rapid succession. "He tried to get me to sign a paper of some sort, but I was so out of it he had to help. He still couldn't get my hand to move properly."

"Do you think you signed it?" Austin asked.

"No. I don't think so."

"Could you read what was on the paper? Do you know what it said?"

"My vision was so blurry, so I really have no idea, but I wonder if it was a document that would give him permission to institutionalize me."

When Keith cocked his head, Austin quickly explained how Dawn believed Noel was trying to make her imagine she was losing her mind. He gave him a few examples.

"What the hell?" Keith shook his head.

One of the most important things Dawn remembered was realizing her marriage was over. "Besides gas lighting and drugging me, I think Noel is somehow involved in the disappearance of Valerie. He wasn't pleased when I told him she and I had lunch together recently."

"Why?" Keith asked.

"Because he probably realized we talked about more than the weather that day. And he would be right. Valerie told me the truth about your family not knowing anything about me or our marriage."

"That's a good motive for retaliation," Keith said. "I hate to say it, but my brother has always been one to hold a grudge. And he holds them forever. His estrangement from me and my parents is proof of that."

"Is anyone else in Thunder Point missing?" Dawn asked Austin.

"No missing person calls have come in. Why do you ask?"

She relayed Noel's phone conversation as she remembered it. "He was speaking to Madeline Reed. I know it was her because he clearly spoke her name, probably thinking I was unconscious. One of the things he told her was something like, 'don't get rid of them.' He said t*hem,* not *her*. He might have been talking about Valerie."

"That comment makes me very nervous," Austin said. "Any guesses as to who else he was referring to?"

She shook her head. "Not unless he was talking about Carl Fisher."

"What's Carl got to do with any of this?"

"Maybe nothing," she admitted, "but I saw him

kissing another woman yesterday when he and Madeline are supposedly an item. Maybe she's the jealous type and she heard he was seeing someone else and flipped out."

"I'll follow all leads," Austin said. "I'll definitely check on Carl Fisher's whereabouts, but my first stop will be Madeline Reed's house." He stood up.

"I'm going with you," Keith said, also standing.

"No, I want you to stay here with Dawn, in case Noel returns. She's not safe with him. He could have killed her last night and he might come back and make sure he succeeds the next time."

She and Keith locked eyes, and he nodded. "Sure, I understand. I don't trust him either. It'll give me and Dawn time to get acquainted."

"Do those guns in your father's den still work?" Austin inquired.

"As far as I know. Noel wouldn't allow me to look at them or take any of them when we closed on the house."

"Noel keeps ammo in the gun cabinet," Dawn offered. "I saw him taking inventory recently. I don't think the cabinet door is locked."

Austin flashed Keith a grave look. "Protect her and yourself by any means." His burning hot gaze met Dawn's, and she felt herself drowning in the depth of his eyes. "I'll be back as soon as I can." With that, he left the room and let himself out the front door.

When she peeked out the curtained window at his exit, she noted his boots sunk into drifts of snow, and it continued to fall heavily from the sky.

CHAPTER THIRTEEN

Keith stomped into Noel's office where Dawn heard him rummaging around. When the loud snap of a shotgun being loaded echoed through the house, she jumped.

"Let me fix some coffee," she offered, filling up the office doorway. "It'll warm us up. It's freezing in this house." She rubbed at the goosebumps peppering her arms.

"That would be great. Thanks. You want me to start a fire in the fireplace?"

"No, I'll just turn the thermostat up." Keith followed her to the hall, where she adjusted the thermostat to a higher temperature and then stepped into the kitchen. When he took a place at the table, she told him about the morning Noel had insisted she'd woken up in the night sweating and asked him to turn the temperature down, though she'd had no memory of it. "That was the first incident of gas lighting." Again, Keith shook his head, unbelieving.

She saw his gaze move around the small space. "Does it seem strange to see another woman moving around your mother's kitchen?" she asked, while putting the coffee on.

He smiled. "A little. My folks lived in this house

their entire lives. Noel and I grew up here, which you probably already know."

She sat across from him to wait for the coffee to perk. The heater in the wall at her feet blew warm air around her ankles, loosening her stiff joints. "Noel hasn't told me much about his growing up. Mostly, he expressed bitterness at your relationship with him and the way you treated your parents. I've since learned that he's told me more lies than truth. He lied to you and your family, too."

"We had no idea he'd married. I wish you could have known my folks. They were good people, even if Pop was a little tough on us boys. It was a generational thing, I guess, the way he tried to instill values with an iron hand. The technique obviously didn't work too well on Noel."

"Did he ever hit either of you?"

"We got the belt across our backsides a few times." He chuckled at the memory. "I'm sure we deserved it."

Dawn doubted that. She didn't believe kids deserved a beating of any kind, no matter what they did wrong. "And your mother?"

"Mom was as sweet as apple pie. She never laid a hand on us. Everyone loved her." He shook his head. "What a waste. Pop was about to retire. They had plans. Life isn't fair, is it, Dawn?"

Thinking of the dreams she'd shared with Noel that had been dashed, she sighed. "Life is what we make it, Keith. We all have free will to do right or wrong, to be happy or let our demons rule us. Noel could have been a wonderful husband and father, if only he'd taken responsibility for his mistakes, moved on from his past, and embraced his life."

"I was the good son," Keith said. "I was always there for my folks when they needed me. In high school, Noel skipped class, got stoned, drank, and generally created havoc. He was kicked off the football team, which about killed my dad, but Pop still tried to help Noel straighten out. A lot of good it did. Noel wanted nothing to do with any advice my parents had to give. He barely graduated high school and then hightailed it off the island for the big city. We'd been estranged from him for years. I don't know why he was so stubborn and unrelenting. Just a bad seed, I guess."

He stopped and contemplated that comment for a moment. Dawn did, too. Noel hadn't been a bad seed when she'd met him. He'd been a perfectly charming man that she fell in love with quickly.

"Not being a part of his life was devastating for my mother," Keith continued. His eyes narrowed into slits. "I'm not sure I can ever forgive him for hurting my folks. And if he's done anything to Val, I'll beat him to a pulp if I get my hands on him." He balled his fists. "I made mistakes in my marriage, but I've changed. I still love Val and would like another chance, if she'll allow me to make it up to her."

"I only met Valerie once, but she seems to have a kind and forgiving heart. Tell me, Keith. Why did you really return to the island? Why now?"

"It's just as Austin said. I came back for Val. When I couldn't reach her after she left me that strange message, I felt in my bones that she was in trouble. I'll do anything to protect her and keep her from harm. Simple as that."

Dawn placed her hand over Keith's, wishing Noel had loved her that much.

"If he's done anything to her..." Keith's voice drifted off.

"We'll both hope for the best."

****

When Austin returned an hour later, Dawn had a steaming cup of coffee ready. He brushed snow off his jacket and stomped clumps off his boots before stepping into the house. Then he flipped his baseball cap off and hung it and his jacket on the coat tree.

"Join us in the kitchen," Dawn said.

The three of them sat at the kitchen table to talk.

"Did you locate Carl Fisher?" she asked.

"Yes. He's safe and sound. Said he and Madeline Reed were not a hot item. He admitted that he was into her more than she was. It just didn't work out and they agreed to move on."

"And you went to Maddie's house? What did she have to say?" Keith inquired.

"She claims not to know anything about Noel's whereabouts. Says the last time she saw him was at the café, the first time she met you, Dawn."

"I distinctly heard Noel call her by name last night. She called him on his cell phone."

"I asked her directly if she'd spoken to him by phone or in person last night, and she looked me straight in the eyes and said there would be no reason for her to be in contact with him."

Dawn shook her head. "Noel told me she always wanted to go to Hollywood to be an actress. She's a good liar."

"She's no Diane Lane, that much is for sure,"

Austin said. "Don't fret. I didn't believe a word out of her mouth."

Relieved, Dawn said, "Good. I'm glad you're not a man who can be easily swayed by a girl's looks."

"I didn't say that." He smiled. "I could be swayed if the right pretty woman set her sights on me, but Maddie Reed is not that person." A muscle quivered in his jaw.

Keith broke the awkward silence that fell between them by standing up and walking to the counter to pour another cup of coffee.

"So, you're a Diane Lane fan, are you?" Dawn said. "I am, too."

"I have a feeling we have more than favorite actors in common." Austin stared at her until she had to look away. "Anyway, I wouldn't be surprised if Noel was hiding in Madeline's house listening behind the door while I was there. I asked if I could go inside and look around, just to satisfy my curiosity. She told me to get a warrant and slammed the door in my face. So, that's what I did. Hopefully, I'll hear from the judge soon. In the meantime, I've got my deputy watching her house."

"Good work, Chief," Keith said.

Austin took a few sips of coffee while holding his gaze on Dawn. "This hits the spot. Weather is getting real nasty outside. Thanks for going to the trouble."

"No trouble, and you're welcome," she replied.

"Have you tried to call Noel on his cell phone?" he asked.

"Yes. As expected, he's not answering. It's going straight to voice mail. I didn't leave a message."

Before Austin could finish the coffee, his radio

crackled. "Chief, this is Deputy Howard. Ms. Reed has just left her house. You want me to follow her?"

"Was she by herself? Could you tell?"

"Couldn't tell. If someone was inside the car, he or she was slumped down in the seat. No one else came out the front door, but her vehicle was pulled to the side of house where someone could have gotten in without my seeing."

"Okay, Brian. Yeah, follow her and let me know where she's headed. I'm on my way to meet you wherever she lands." He swallowed the last bit of coffee and strode to the foyer to throw on his jacket.

"I'm going with you," Keith said. "If Maddie's got Val, I want to be there."

"Let me go, too," Dawn said. "Noel is my husband, and he's put me in the middle of this mess." She was already shoving her feet into hiking boots and her arms into her coat sleeves. She wrapped a scarf around her neck and jammed a knit cap over her head.

"Absolutely not." Austin halted her by locking his hands on her arms. "It's too dangerous. We have no idea if Noel is even with Maddie. If he is, one or both of them could be armed. I won't take the chance of you getting hurt. Either of you."

"I can't stay here and wonder what's happening. Please let me go. I won't get in the way."

Myriad reactions crossed his face before he grudgingly relented. "All right, it might be better for you to be with me than here by yourself, in case Noel comes back home with more malice on his mind." He nodded at Keith. "You both can go, but you have to stay in my truck. I know it's personal for you both, but this is police business. You understand?"

Both Dawn and Keith nodded their agreement. Austin grabbed his cap from the coat tree and snugged it over his scalp. The three of them left the house and trudged through the snow to Austin's police truck. He opened the door to the passenger side, and Dawn slid across the seat to sit in the middle. Keith climbed in beside her.

As Austin drove toward town, the car radio crackled to life again. "Chief, Maddie Reed is headed to the State Park."

"Stay on her trail without her catching sight of you, Brian. I'll meet you there."

"Will do."

Several times the truck slid in the slick snow, causing Dawn to suck in breath and press her palms against the dashboard for support. After driving down Main Street and past the ferry landing and gazebo, Austin turned off on the Island Trail Head road. With snow continuing to fall, the road sure looked different from the day she'd gone down it with Noel. The six miles to the park entrance and parking lot were six of the longest she'd ever traveled.

Only two cars were in the lot when they arrived; one was a police car with chains on the tires. Austin pulled beside it and rolled down his window to speak to his deputy, who rolled his window down.

"Noel Matheson is with Maddie, Chief. They went down the trail toward the ice caves."

"Did they see you?"

"No, sir."

"All right. Let's find out what they're up to."

"In this weather, it's gotta be no good," Brian replied.

Both men rolled their windows back up. Austin glanced between Dawn and Keith. "You two stay here like you promised. I'll keep the truck running with the heater going."

They nodded and he closed the door behind him. Dawn leaned forward and watched through the windshield as he and his deputy crossed the wooden bridge suspended over the river. When Austin slipped, Dawn let out a gasp. Luckily, he caught himself on the hand railing before he could fall.

When the men were out of sight, Keith announced, "I'm not staying here," and he opened the passenger door.

"We promised Austin," Dawn reminded him.

"They could be holding Val captive in those caves. She might be close to death in this weather. Besides, the chief and his deputy might need my help." He showed her the revolver tucked in his coat pocket.

"Well, I'm not staying here alone." She switched the ignition off and deposited the keys in her coat pocket. "I'm going with you."

She slipped and nearly fell as she and Keith trudged their way across the bridge and over the snow-covered boardwalk.

"This way to the caves," he said, leading her to a side trail that meandered along Lake Superior. The cliffs along the lake had formed crimson red borders creating an arctic landscape. Pillars of ice extended to the cliff tops where waterfalls had hardened in place. Gasping at the natural beauty, Dawn inhaled a frigid breath into her lungs.

After an almost 1-mile hike over ground that was slippery, bumpy, and filled with snow cracks and ice and snow mounds, they finally neared the entrance to the caves. Exhausted, Dawn's cheeks and nose felt frozen. Keith stuck his arm out and put a finger to his lips, warning her to keep quiet. Austin and Brian were just ahead, poised at the cave opening with their guns drawn.

Dawn stared at the huge opening into a cave formation that could only be described as a fairyland of sparkling needle-like icicles that hung from the ceiling and jutted up from the ground below. Thick, glistening ice blanketed the inside walls.

When she shifted from one numb foot to the other, the snow beneath her boots crunched. Austin's head turned, and the look on his face expressed a mixture of concern, exasperation, and disappointment. Dawn's lungs deflated, feeling terrible for having broken her promise to stay in the truck.

He motioned for them to stay where they were.

Noel's voice boomed from out of the cave, nearly stopping Dawn's heart.

"I never wanted anyone to get hurt, Maddie. You know that!"

Madeline's retort was angry. "Too late. These two bitches know too much. They'll destroy us and ruin our future."

"Why did you have to involve Val? I don't want my sister-in-law's blood on my hands."

Dawn felt Keith tense beside her. She grabbed his arm and held tight to keep him from vaulting forward. Maddie had said 'these two.' Who was the other person she referred to?

"And, apparently, you didn't want any of your wife's blood on you either, did you?" Madeline mocked, her voice raised. "I wish you would have gotten rid of her that day you brought her out here to the cliffs."

"I never intended to hurt Dawn. That was an accident. The plan was to isolate her from everyone she knew and cared about, feed on her depression, and scare her into thinking she'd lost her mind."

"And lock her away after she'd signed over her inheritance to you," Madeline said.

"That's right. If she'd gone over the cliff that day before signing the documents, we'd have nothing."

Dawn's heart dropped to her stomach, feeling like a piece of granite. Money. That's what all of this had been about. Noel wanted her money. Obviously, he wanted Madeline, too. In order to have both, he'd been willing to lock Dawn away for the rest of her life.

"Once these two are dead," Maddie went on, "your only job is to get your wife to sign her fortune over to you and then make her death look like an accident or suicide. I'm tired of waiting for her to be out of our lives."

Feeling her knees buckle, Dawn sunk to the cold ground. Austin had been right when he'd said those closest to us cut deep. Had Noel ever loved her, or had their entire marriage been a sham?

Keith knelt next to her. Dawn felt his arm around her at the same time her gaze met Austin's across the frozen tundra. It held sympathy and something deeper and darker—fury. Apparently, he'd heard enough. He motioned to Brian, and they both cocked their guns and moved as quickly as was possible into the cave without giving Noel and Madeline warning of their approach. Dawn watched as they descended what she'd soon discover were ice steps.

"Raise your hands and then don't move!" Austin shouted.

Keith grabbed Dawn's hand and dragged her to the mouth of the cave just in time to see Maddie spin.

The blast from the revolver she held echoed like the crack of a whip. Dawn screamed when she saw Austin fall. Before Maddie could get off another shot, Brian's gun exploded, hitting her in the leg. She grunted and collapsed to the ground. Her gun fell from her hand, sliding over the ice to land a few feet from Austin. Noel lurched for it, but came up short and landed hard on his shoulder. The young deputy sprang into action, scrambling over the slick ice. When Noel reached for and grabbed the gun, Brian kicked it out of his hand. As Noel yelped in pain, Brian grabbed the gun from off the ground and de-cocked it.

He roughly shoved Noel onto his stomach and snapped handcuffs onto his wrists, leaving him face down. As Madeline started crawling past the unconscious Austin, Keith jumped into action. He clambered down the steep ice steps, leaped into the air, and tackled her. She groaned when his heavy body landed on hers. Clamping his arms securely around her, the two of them slid a couple of feet across the ice. Dawn watched from the steps as Keith manhandled the squirming woman and flipped her onto her stomach just as Brian had done to Noel.

"I got her, Deputy!"

"Good job, Mr. Matheson. Hold onto her a minute longer." Brian shuffled over to Austin and shook him. Austin's eyes rolled open. "You alive, Chief?"

Austin nodded.

"Glad to hear it. I'm gonna need your handcuffs, sir." Austin nodded and fumbled around in his coat pocket for a pair and handed them to Brian. "Thanks, Chief. The male suspect is already cuffed. I'll truss the woman up and then radio for help."

"Good work," Austin replied.

Brian squeezed Madeline's wrists together and locked the cuffs.

"You shot me, you sonofabitch. I need a doctor," she snapped.

"Unfortunately, you'll get it," he replied, dryly.

Knowing there would be no more gunshots fired, Dawn carefully made her way down the precipitous steps and skated to Austin to help him to sit up. A ragged hole gaped from the sleeve of his bomber jacket, blood already drying in the mind-numbing cold. She couldn't tell how badly he was injured.

"You were shot," she said, trying to keep her voice calm.

"Yeah, but it's just a nick. The good thing is, it's so damn cold I can barely feel the pain." His mouth tipped in a slow smile.

She helped him to stand, and he nodded at Brian. "I'm proud of the way you handled this situation, Deputy."

"Thanks, Chief. We also owe the other Mr. Matheson a big thank you. He captured the woman." As soon as the words exited his mouth, Dawn glanced around and realized Keith wasn't among them.

"Where is he?" she asked.

His voice echoed over the ice. "Over here, Chief! Hurry!"

Dawn pointed to Keith, who was madly waving at

them from what looked like a smaller cave entrance about thirty feet away.

Austin, Brian, and Dawn half skated, half jogged to him.

"It's Val and another woman! They're here," Keith said, ducking under a low hanging chunk of ice.

Slumped against each other on the ground was Valerie and Leslie, Madeline's friend. Both were gagged with their arms tied behind their backs. Neither were wearing cold weather gear and were pale and looked near death.

"Deputy, get on the radio and call for an ambulance, and tell them to double-time it," Austin ordered.

"Yes, sir." Brian took off.

Dawn and Keith removed Valerie and Leslie's gags as fast as possible. Then Keith extracted a pocket knife from his jeans pocket and carefully broke the ropes cutting into Val's wrists first and then Leslie's. Valerie's face winced in pain. Leslie's eyes remained closed.

"Oh, Valerie." Tears sprang into Dawn's eyes but immediately began to harden on her cheeks. She gently hugged the woman, afraid of hurting her.

"I...I..." Val's lips were so cracked and chapped, they were bleeding.

"Don't try to talk," Keith told her. Handling them like fragile eggs, he sat both women up. Val tried to wiggle her hands, but Leslie didn't move at all.

"Is she...?" Dawn hesitated.

Austin removed his glove and placed two fingers against her neck. "There's a pulse but it's weak. They both need medical attention immediately." When he heard the clomp of boots pounding on ice, he glanced over his shoulder to see Brian returning.

"Ambulance and paramedics are on their way," Brian said.

Keith removed his coat and snugged it around Valerie and then nestled as close to her as possible, wrapping his arm around her shoulders. Unable to speak, she let her head loll on his shoulder.

"Help me out of my jacket," Austin said to Dawn.

"Is that a good idea? With your wound, you could go into shock."

"Leslie needs the warmth more than I do."

Although she suspected Leslie was not completely innocent in all that had transpired, Dawn did as he asked, being extra careful as she tugged the sleeve down his wounded arm. When the jacket was off, she put it around Leslie, who still didn't open her eyes.

After what seemed like an eternity, sirens echoed in the distance. Eventually, six paramedics entered the cave hauling medical boxes and three stretchers. When they stopped at Madeline and Noel's bodies, Austin waved them over. "We have two women over here who need taken care of fist!" he hollered.

The medical team made quick work of checking each woman's vitals and then attached them to IV's, loaded them onto the stretchers, and covered them with heated blankets. They returned Austin and Keith's coats to them, and the stretchers were carried by two paramedics each. They carefully climbed the ice steps out of the cave. It would be a long and dangerous hike back to the lot where the ambulance was parked.

"What about me?" Madeline cried. "I'm shot and need attention." She and Noel were both shaking uncontrollably. It had to be freezing on the ground lying face down that way. Dawn hoped they got frost bite.

"Deputy, arrest them both and read them their rights," Austin told Brian.

"Sure thing, Chief. On what charges?"

"Attempted murder, kidnapping, harassment, and anything else you think we can make stick." His dark gaze shifted between Madeline and Noel's prone bodies.

She twisted her head and screamed, "Let me up!"

"What happened to her?" one of the paramedics asked, opening his medical box.

"I shot her in the leg," Brian answered, nonchalantly.

None so gently, Austin shoved his foot under her rib and rolled her over. She grunted and screeched about police brutality.

"Shut up or I'll shoot you in your other leg," Austin warned. With fire in his eyes, he then hauled Noel up by the collar using his good arm. "You got any complaints, Mr. Matheson?"

Glaring, Noel shook his head.

"I didn't think so." Austin turned and met Dawn's gaze. "You want to say anything to him before we haul him away?"

There were so many things she wanted to know and might never get the answers to. But now was not the time for questions. She strode to Noel and stared into his eyes. His face was blank, his eyes cold and unapologetic. Any bit of love she'd been holding onto vanished like dust in the wind.

Never wanting to utter another word to the man

who had betrayed her in so many ways, she let her hand do the talking. Two sharp slaps across his face left stinging red imprints on both of his cheeks.

"Ow! That hurt!" he exclaimed, narrowing his eyes.

"Your pain is just beginning," Austin said. He nodded to the paramedics. "Do what you have to do and get the two of them out of here. Take them straight to the jail."

Once the medical team wrapped her leg, they heaved Madeline onto the stretcher and started up the ice steps with Brian and Noel following. Brian prodded his prisoner in the back.

Austin turned to Dawn. "Are you okay?"

"I will be."

He nodded.

"We need to get you to the clinic, too," she said, drawing her arm around his waist.

"That's probably a good idea," he admitted. "I'm starting to feel a little woozy."

She helped him up the ice stairs and started them walking down the snow-covered trail. Why don't you use your radio to call the ambulance and ask them to wait for us?"

"I don't need the ambulance."

The strong tilt of his chin spoke volumes about his courage and pain tolerance. "In that case, are there any laws against a private citizen driving your police truck?" she asked.

"None that I'm aware of. Why?"

She retrieved his car keys from her pocket and jingled them. "Because today I'm your chauffeur."

CHAPTER FOURTEEN

Two Weeks Later

Dawn entered the police station after receiving a call from Austin asking her to come see him. He had news. She removed her hat and gloves and unbuttoned her coat. Outside the weather was cold and dreary, but inside the police station, the temperature was as warm as toast.

Mary Beth, the station's very pregnant receptionist, welcomed her with a smile and buzzed Austin to let him know she had arrived. "Go on in," she said, hooking her thumb in the direction of his office.

"Good afternoon," he greeted from the desk he was now relegated to. Despite having undergone shoulder surgery and his arm in a sling, he looked to be in great spirits.

"Hello, Austin. What a nice smile you have today. You look happy."

"I am. For a cop sitting at a desk in a sling, anyway. Don't I always have a smile on my face when you're around?"

She grinned and took a seat in a straight wooden chair across from his desk.

"You're looking mighty pretty today. Like a ray of sunshine on this gray and gloomy day." His gaze lingered, causing her to blush at his compliment.

Not having done anything special to her usual hair and makeup routine, Austin made her feel beautiful and desired—something she hadn't felt in a long time. It was the way in which he looked at her—really looked at her, as if he wanted to dip her in sugar and eat her up.

In the past two weeks since all hell had broken loose, they'd spent almost every day together. The day after Noel and Madeline were arrested, Dawn traveled to Big Bay and held vigil in the waiting room during Austin's surgery. Since his return to Wolf Island, she'd cooked him dinner most nights and brought him lunch most days. After all, it was difficult for him to cook with one arm in a sling.

They'd enjoyed hours of conversation and discovered they had much more in common than favorite actors.

While hedging around their growing attraction, Austin seemed as pleased to spend time with her as she was with him. Despite their increasing closeness, he had never crossed the line. Austin had been a perfect gentleman. They hadn't even kissed, not that Dawn hadn't imagined what it'd be like.

He'd been in Big Bay for the last few days working the case, and it had surprised her how much she'd missed him, his positive attitude, and friendly demeanor in that short time. While he was gone, Dawn had attended to several important matters. She was anxious to tell him what she'd accomplished while he was off island, but first things first.

"Did you see the doctor this morning?" she asked, wanting to know about his progress before hearing what he'd called her in for.

"Yeah, I'll probably have to wear this sling for another two or three weeks, but strength in my arm is improving now that I've started physical therapy."

"That's great. You're a strong man and will heal quickly."

He nodded. "What's not so great is sitting at this desk all day delegating duties. I like being out in the field."

"Anxious to get shot at again, are you?" she teased. "Don't rush it. You'll be back to pounding the pavement before you know it."

"Coffee?" he asked, standing to refill his cup.

"No thanks, I had some already." She inhaled a breath. "You have news for me?"

He didn't hesitate. "Yes, I do. Leslie Duvall is finally well enough to talk, and she's had a whole lot to say."

So far, while awaiting court dates in Big Bay, neither Noel nor Madeline had confessed to any wrongdoing, which was ridiculous, of course, since they'd been caught red-handed holding Valerie and Leslie captive. It still seemed a clear-cut case, but one never knew about the justice system and whether it would work.

Dawn clutched the arms of the chair and felt her heart rate pick up. "I'm listening."

Austin paraphrased from the notes he'd received from a recent interview Leslie had given from her hospital bed. "Madeline and Noel saw each other for the first time in years when he returned to Thunder

Point for Betty and Tom's funeral. Apparently, he'd had a crush on her in high school, and when they met up again, they hit it off in a big way and immediately began an affair." He stopped to gauge her reaction.

Having already figured as much, the pain of hearing the truth still caused Dawn's chest to ache like she'd been stabbed with a hot poker. "Go on," she said.

"After Noel told Madeline about your miscarriages, the depression that followed, and his growing unhappiness, he admitted to her that he wished there was some way to get out of his marriage. He'd fallen in love with Madeline and wanted to be with her. Divorce from you was not an option, because of your family fortune. If you divorced, he knew he'd never get his hands on your inheritance."

Again, he halted and met her gaze. Dawn had already told him that she'd suffered the two miscarriages and had sunk into a depression. She'd also shared that she felt stronger and happier than ever, despite Noel having tried to ruin her life.

Austin continued. "Once Maddie learned about your money, the two of them hatched a plan—the plan we heard them discuss in the ice caves. As we know, the idea behind the gas lighting was to make you think you were imagining things so that you'd have a breakdown and completely lose your mind. Because of your past bouts of depression, they figured they'd be able to find, or pay off, a crooked doctor who would institutionalize you—after you signed over your inheritance to Noel."

She shook her head. "What was the howling wolf about, and the dead animal on the porch step?"

"Just more scare tactics to drive you mad. Tactics that led to a more devious idea, unfortunately. Madeline had a recording of a howling wolf that she played through speakers in the woods. As for the dog, she killed that animal herself and placed it on the porch step knowing exactly when you and Noel would arrive home that day. She dated Carl Fisher, a vet technician at the veterinarian's office here in town, just long enough to gain access to the Pentobarbital that she used to euthanize the dog. Apparently, the poor animal was a stray she found on the road. Then she used a handmade trap with claws to make it look like the dog's throat had been ripped out. Her father was a welder when he was alive and he'd taught her the trade as a girl. She made the trap herself." Austin paused. "According to Leslie, Madeline wanted you out of the picture completely, just as soon as you signed over your inheritance to Noel. Because they'd planted the idea that wolves had returned to the island, using the trap would make the attack on you look like a wolf attack." Austin waited for that to sink in.

Dawn could barely respond for several moments. "Do you mean to say that committing me to a psychiatric ward was not enough for her? She wanted me dead, and using her homemade trap was how she planned to murder me?"

He nodded. "Fortunately, when she made that suggestion to Noel, he rejected it." Austin's lips pursed and his chest heaved. "He's a bastard, but she's a real sick piece of work."

Silence danced around them for a few beats. Once they both regained composure, Dawn asked, "Why did they kidnap Valerie?"

"Simple. Noel was afraid Valerie would continue to tell you the truth about him, and perhaps even convince you to leave him before he got what he wanted. Madeline decided she was too big of a threat and had to be silenced. Madeline, apparently, is not a patient person."

"Poor Valerie. Why did Madeline involve Leslie in any of her and Noel's plans? I thought they were friends."

"Leslie was weak. Madeline used her to do some of their dirty work. She was the one who dressed like a ghost in the woods, played the recording of the crying baby, and hit you over the head. Madeline and Noel promised her a big chunk of cash for participating in their evil plot. We discovered, and she finally admitted, that she has a gambling problem, is up to her eyeballs in debt, and was about to file bankruptcy and lose everything she owned. She was willing to do whatever Madeline wanted for money. But after hearing you were in a coma and thinking she'd killed you, her conscience kicked in. When she confronted Madeline to stop and abandon their plans, Maddie would have none of it. They got into an argument and Leslie threatened to come to me and tell me everything. That's when Madeline decided to get rid of her, too."

"I saw them arguing the day I got out of the clinic," Dawn said. "What a nightmare."

"It sure is a nightmare, and I may have seen something like it on a Lifetime movie." Austin's eyes twinkled with mischief.

She couldn't help but smile at his attempt to lighten the mood. "There are still things I don't understand. Noel was pushing for me to get pregnant up until a few weeks ago. He wanted to be a father so badly. It was all he talked about for such a long time. Or at least that's what he led me to believe. Every time we lost a baby, he acted like he was devastated. I was too wrapped up in my own loss and guilt to offer him much comfort. I suppose he was more deeply affected than I realized."

"Don't think for even one minute that any of this was your fault," Austin said.

"As I've told you, it was Noel's idea to move to Wolf Island," she said. "He claimed a change of scenery would, in his words, help me to relax and get pregnant. I went along with it because our relationship was in such a bad way. I hoped we could eventually grow closer again, even when I was pushing him away. Now I realize he just wanted to be close to Madeline." She took a deep breath. "Suddenly, he said he didn't think we should bring a child into the world because of my *issues*. It came out of nowhere."

Austin replied quietly. "Because he found out he was getting what he wanted."

Her eyes widened with comprehension.

Austin nodded affirmation. "Madeline Reed is pregnant with his child. That's one of the reasons they were trying to get you committed as soon as possible. She wanted Noel to marry her."

Dawn held her head in her hands. When she lifted her gaze, she said, "Keith told me Noel never felt he lived up to their father's expectations. That's why he rebelled growing up and then estranged himself from the family when he was old enough to leave home. I suppose that's why he never told them about me or our marriage. He still held a grudge."

"That's a long time to hold a grudge," Austin noted.

"I'm no psychiatrist, but I'm guessing it was his way of maintaining control. And he apparently blames me for the things in his life that haven't gone right. I refused to let him touch my inheritance money and I couldn't get pregnant." She sighed. "The thing is, I married a good man. At least, he was good to me in the beginning. I must have been naïve or stupid, since I suppose all he ever wanted from me was my money."

Austin stood up and moved to her side. He placed his hand on her shoulder. "You're neither naïve or stupid. Noel probably did love you. His folks were good people. They raised him just fine. Somewhere along the way he became selfish and greedy and was blind to all the good in his life. He has demons, but they have nothing to do with you."

"Thank you for saying that, Austin. I know you're right. And I don't blame myself for anything he did."

He stood in front of her and leaned his backside against the desk. "He and Madeline will both be locked up for life if they're convicted, and I've no doubt they'll be convicted. The evidence was overwhelming even before Leslie gave her statement. Her confession will seal their destiny."

"What's going to happen to Leslie?" Dawn asked.

"The D.A. cut her a deal for handing them to us, but she'll still do time for her assault on you."

Dawn nodded, feeling that was fair.

"For what it's worth, she wanted you to know how sorry she is and asked for your forgiveness."

"I'm not someone who withholds forgiveness,

Austin. Leslie does need to own her part, but I appreciate that she's come forward so that Noel and Madeline will be dealt with and justice will be served."

"That's generous of you, considering she could have killed you."

"She'll have her own demons to live with for the rest of her life."

Several more beats passed before Austin spoke again. "What will you do now, Dawn? Do you plan on staying here in Thunder Point, or will you be returning to Chicago?"

Though they'd had many conversations, this was a subject they hadn't had courage to delve into. Both had skirted the subject. Despite their obvious attraction, she was married, and Wolf Island held memories that were far from pleasant. Her friends were in Chicago, and she was confident she could get her old job back at the thrift store.

"I haven't decided yet," she answered truthfully, "but I've already spoken to a divorce attorney and filed papers. The final decree should be signed in four to five months."

Surprise illuminated Austin's features, and he grinned with satisfaction.

"What's happening with the Matheson house?" he asked.

"Keith wants it. Turns out he always wanted it. That's what he and Noel fought about at their parents' funeral. Noel tried to draw things out so he could continue coming back here, where he could be with Madeline. He made life so difficult about splitting the property that Keith gave up and left the island. He said his brother had been so problematic for so many years, and he was tired of it. Now that Noel is no longer standing in his way, I'm happy for Keith to have the house. I've started proceedings to transfer the deed to him."

"What about Noel? The house and property belongs to him. Doesn't he need to agree on transferring the deed?"

"Not if he's convicted."

"And we both know that's going to happen," Austin repeated with confidence. "You're full of surprises today, aren't you?"

"I have another one for you. While you were in Big Bay, I moved to the Antler Motel so Keith and Valerie could go ahead and settle in. I didn't see a point in waiting. Besides, I never felt comfortable in that house."

"Valerie is moving in with him?" Austin asked.

"Yes. They both acknowledge the mistakes they made in their marriage and are willing to work at changing. The two of them are going to give their relationship another try."

He smiled. "That's great. I like them both. How is she doing, physically?"

"As you know, she lost a toe to frost bite, and she's still experiencing tingling and numbness in her hands. She's grateful to be alive. It could have been so much worse. Physical therapy is helping."

"A lot has happened since I've been gone," he said.

"Yes, it has." What she felt at that moment was comfort at his presence and recognition of a vague, restless unhappiness when he wasn't around. The emotion ran deep and quiet and true.

When he reached for her hand, she gave it

willingly. His touch sent a sizzle through her veins. His thumb rubbed the inside of her palm—the gesture unexpected and intimate. She thought to herself, 'I could love this man.' The words came unbidden in her mind and the realization was so authentic and dear.

His voice dropped low. "You know, Mary Beth is having that baby soon and will be on maternity leave for several months. I'm going to need a receptionist to fill in while she's out. Would you be interested in the job?"

He spoke with such tenderness that it brought unexpected tears to her eyes. She let the thought roll around in her mind.

"While I very much appreciate the offer, I've been in touch with Evie. She asked if I'll consider staying at her house and taking care of the horses while she recovers from knee surgery."

He squeezed her hand tighter. "You like working with horses?"

"I didn't have much of an opportunity, but I want to give it another try. Evie's going to be at the rehabilitation center for at least four more weeks, and she'll still need help after she returns home."

"You're a good person, Dawn."

"Evie is a good person. She was my first friend here. I'd do anything to help her."

"So, does that mean you've just made your decision to stay in Thunder Point?" His eyes lit with hope and passion.

Her lips tilted in a coy smile. "I'd like to experience the island in the summer time. I hear it's beautiful here that time of year."

He gently pulled her to her feet, pulled her close

to his chest, and gazed so longingly at her that her heart nearly stopped beating. "From here, the view is the most beautiful I've ever seen."

She looked at him wordlessly, breathlessly, safe and content in his arms—absolutely sure that this was the right place for her, with this man, at this time.

ABOUT THE AUTHOR

Stacey Coverstone wrote her first novel in 2006 after an inspiring week at Cowgirl Camp in New Mexico, a gift from her husband for earning her Master's degree. When that western romance was quickly accepted for publication, there was no looking back. She now writes in several genres, including western romance, romantic suspense, Gothic romance, and mysteries and ghost stories. Stacey is also a freelance fiction editor, who likes working with new, Indie, and established authors.

To view all of Stacey's books, or to get information on her editing services, please visit her website at: www.staceycoverstone.com.

You can also find her on Facebook.

You might be interested in her first "Secrets" book: *SECRETS OF SEACLIFF HOUSE*, available at Amazon and in print.

Stacey and her husband call the charming lakeside town of Mount Dora, Florida home, where she works in Special Events Sales at the historic (and some say *haunted*) 1883 Lakeside Inn. In her off time, she enjoys the beach, bicycle riding, camping, traveling, photography, target shooting, and her rescue dog, Buster.

If you enjoyed this book, please take a few moments to write a short review on Amazon and any other review site you participate in. Letting others know you enjoyed a book is a quick and easy way to champion an author's work.

Thank you!

Made in the USA
Columbia, SC
06 November 2025